Deal BREAKERS

LAURA LEE

Part
ONE

The College Years

ONE

FRESHMAN YEAR

RILEY

"HOLY FUCKING SHIT, DUDE. Hot blonde at two o'clock," Josh, my new dormmate says.

I look and I'm stunned. Hot is a major understatement for the blonde beauty standing by the bike racks. She's magnificent. I know that's a total chick word to use but it's the only thing that comes to mind. I've never seen something so incredible. I watch as she secures her bike to the rack and walks away with her beat up backpack slung over her shoulder. The girl is a walking contradiction. She's wearing a simple t-shirt and jeans but she looks like she just stepped off a runway. Instead of using some giant, impractical, yet fashionable bag like most girls around campus, she's carrying something plain and perfectly functional. I step closer and notice that her bike is one of those old-fashioned ones with a straw basket in the front and the frame is covered in hand-painted flowers. It definitely stands out amongst the rest. Just like its owner.

"Wow," I say.

I have to meet this girl. And I don't know why, but I feel like I have to make a big impression and I'm at a loss on how to do it. I don't want to sound cocky, but I'm one of those dudes that has never really had to work for it. I was one of the lucky ones who shot up ten inches right before my freshman year of high school. At six foot two and athletic pretty much my entire life, no one ever messed with me. I was always in the popular crowd and I never went through an awkward phase like most teenagers do. I have good looks and good skin and yeah, I'll admit, I've used that to my advantage. Hell, I've only been on campus at the University of Oregon for a week and I've already had a few hookups. It just comes easily for me. I can tell this girl is different though —she'll be a challenge—but I'd bet my entire academic scholarship that the reward will be *so* worth the effort.

Josh and I walk our bikes to the rack and begin the process of locking them up. I smile when I come up with a brilliant plan to introduce myself to her. I slide my front wheel next to hers and *accidentally* loop my chain around both her frame and mine. There's no way she's getting away without talking to me first.

Josh smirks when he sees what I'm doing. "Well, that's a new approach. I don't think I've ever heard of taking someone's bike hostage to get a date."

I shrug. "I'm hoping the originality of it will earn me some points."

He slaps me on the back. "C'mon Rye, we're going to be late for Chem."

After Chem Lab, I wait in the green space next to the bike racks trying not to look like a creepy stalker. I don't want to risk pissing off the hot blonde from earlier by making her late for class or something so I'm sitting here like a schmuck waiting for her. I stand up tall when I see her approach her bike and notice right away what I've done. She has this adorable little crinkle in her brow and she bites her sexy lip as she assesses the situation. She tugs on the cable and lets out a big huff.

I surreptitiously check out her amazing body as I sidle up to her. "Hi there. It looks like you're having an issue, huh?"

She sighs. "Ugh, some idiot locked their bike to mine. I'm going to be late for class if I have to walk across campus to get there."

"I think I can help you," I say.

Her round, hazel eyes brighten. "Really? How are you going to do that?"

I start working the combination on my lock and catch her eyes as she makes the connection. I stand up and offer my hand in greeting. "I'm Riley McIntyre. Also known as the *idiot*."

She laughs and shakes my hand. "Devyn. Devyn Summers. So tell me, Riley, why on earth would you lock our bikes together?"

I smile and decide to go with honesty. "I saw you earlier and...I don't know...felt that I had to meet you. You ran off so quickly that this was the only thing I could think of."

She raises a perfectly sculpted eyebrow. "And why did you feel like you *had* to meet me?"

I shrug. "A bunch of people from my dorm are meeting at The Duck Pond later for the game. I wanted to invite you."

"Isn't that the sports bar over on University Street?"

I nod. "It is. They have big screens, a few pool tables, darts, and cheap beer. It's a pretty cool place to hang out."

She bites her lip again. "Oh. I'm not old enough to drink. I'm only a freshman."

"So am I," I say. "But it's cool. It's a pub so it's open to

all ages. Some of the upperclassmen buy pitchers and we all
share. They only check your ID if you're buying."

"We've only been on campus a week. How do you know
this already?"

I laugh. "An old football buddy of mine from high school
is a junior. He's been showing me the ropes. So, are you in?
Kickoff is at five so we'll all head over there shortly
beforehand."

"The Niners game?" she asks.

"Yeah, I'm looking forward to seeing them get their asses
kicked."

She frowns. "Puh-leez. The Seahawks are a decent team,
but they're not so impressive when they're not at home with
all their twelfth man loud stadium garbage. Niners totally
have this one."

Holy shit, this chick knows football? "I disagree. Wilson
has been in top shape this season."

She smirks. "So has Kaepernick."

I may have just jizzed in my pants a little. How can a
woman this hot possibly know football? I think I'm in love.
"You willing to put your money where your mouth is?"

She backs her bike out of the rack and straddles it.
"What did you have in mind?"

I picture her straddling my face instead as I pull my bike
out too. "For every Seahawks touchdown, you owe me a
beer. I'll do the same for you *if* the Niners ever get one."

She glares at me. "Oh, you're so on! But make mine
soda."

My mouth quirks at that. So she's not a rule breaker,
huh? I'll have to see what I can do about that. "It's a date."

She frowns. "No, not a date. We're just going to…hang
out."

I mirror her expression. "What's wrong with a date? Do
you have a boyfriend?"

She shakes her head. "No, no boyfriend. I'm just not looking for a date right now."

I feign nonchalance. "That's cool. We can totally just hang."

She perks up again. "Really? You'd be okay with that? I don't want to give you the wrong impression—I mean what I say—I'm just looking for a friend. Nothing more."

Man, she's going to be tougher to crack than I thought. "It's totally fine. I could always use more friends. The more the merrier, right?"

Her face lights up in a smile as she turns her bike towards the other end of campus. "Right. I'll meet you there around five. I need to get to class."

"See you then," I say as I watch her pedal away.

MY BUDDY ADAM AND I are playing pool when she walks in. "Day-um," he says as he watches her coming towards us.

"Dibs," I call as I set the pool stick down. "I'm done playing, man. This is my date." Whether Devyn wants to call it one or not, this dickhead needs to know she's off limits.

She smiles as I approach her. "Hi, Riley." She looks around. "You're right; this place is pretty cool."

My eyes run the length of her body. She's wearing the same jeans from earlier but she's changed into a form-fitting 49ers t-shirt. Her tits are a little on the small side but they're nicely rounded and perky. I find myself wondering what shade of pink her nipples are. She clears her throat, probably because I'm staring at her chest. I lift my eyes and say, "Nice shirt."

She looks down. "Thanks. It's my lucky shirt. They win every time I wear it."

I laugh as I take her hand and lead her to a table in the back. "Oh yeah? Well, good call because they need all the help they can get."

She glances at our joined hands and blushes. "So you say. We'll see." She pulls her hand away and takes a seat.

I take the chair directly across from her. I deliberately chose a two-top so the assholes that are currently checking her out get the message to leave us alone.

I raise the pitcher of beer that I set down earlier and pour a glass. "You want one?"

She gulps. "No, thank you."

I smile. "Oh, that's right, you're more of a soda girl. What can I get for you?"

"Pepsi or Coke is fine," she says.

I make a quick run to the bar and return with a glass of Pepsi. I place it in front of her with a dramatic bow. "Your soda, milady."

She laughs. "Well, aren't you the quintessential gentleman? Does that crap normally work for you?"

I take my seat and return her laughter. "Usually, yeah."

She snorts. "Well, Romeo, you can save the charm for later. We're here as *friends*. Remember?"

"Right," I say. "So, you like football, huh?"

She nods enthusiastically. "Oh yeah. I like every sport really, but football is definitely my favorite. I watched religiously with my dad and brother growing up. On Sundays, we worshipped at the Church of the Flying Pigskin. My mom made the best nachos for us. It was great."

"What are you doing after this?" I ask. "You wanna get married? Because seriously, you are like my dream woman."

She laughs. "Ah, sorry, but I'm not looking for dates *or* husbands today. Tough luck there, Romeo."

"So where's home for you?" I ask, trying not to count how many times she's shot me down already.

"Ashland, Oregon. It's a few hours south of here right above the California border."

"Yeah, I'm familiar," I say. "I'm from Napa. My mom used to drag me up to the Shakespeare Festival every year when I was younger. She wanted to expose me to some culture or shit like that. Personally, the five hour drive was a pain in my ass. I finally convinced her that I had enough culture when I started high school."

She laughs. "Oh, you're totally missing out. I've been countless times and it never gets old."

"I'll take your word for it," I laugh.

"We'll have to go together sometime. Seriously. If you don't like it, you just haven't had the right experience yet."

My dick perks up at this. She's already talking about future outings. Taking me with her to her hometown. Normally, I'd say she was getting way too clingy but I'm not getting that vibe from her. I sip my beer and nod. "I might just take you up on that. Maybe we can check it out when we go home for the summer. I can easily make a pit stop in Ashland."

She ducks her head. "I'm not going home for the summer."

"What? Why not? It's so close. Wouldn't your parents be pissed?"

"I don't have parents," she whispered.

"What? But you just said—"

She looks up and her eyes are a little shiny. *What the hell?* "They died. My mom...she had breast cancer. It took her when I was ten. Then my dad...he had a heart attack halfway through my senior year of high school. He went to bed one night and never woke up. It's just me and my brother now. He's almost four years older so he came to help me through graduation but then he moved to Seattle last month."

Oh shit. I have no idea what to say. She just exposed something so personal and raw. I want to pull her into the world's biggest bear hug but for some reason, I think she'd fight that. I reach across the table and settle for a hand squeeze. "I'm sorry for your loss, Devyn. Really. That really sucks."

DEVYN

HOLY CRAP, WHY DID I just blurt that out to a virtual stranger? I can't believe I told him about my parents! I came to U of O so I wouldn't be the poor orphan that everyone back home considered me to be. Being in Eugene was my chance at a fresh start and I just blew it by telling this guy I just met about them. What the heck was I thinking? What is it about this guy that makes me feel like baring my soul? He's obviously a huge player which is not even close to my type. But God, sitting here with him, I feel like I've known him forever.

Trying to lighten the mood, I nod towards his beer and say, "I've changed my mind. Can I try a sip?"

He looks skeptical but he hands the mug over. "Sure."

I hesitantly take a sip and actually like it. I've heard that beer is an acquired taste, but this stuff is *yummy*. I take a large gulp. "Wow, this is good. I've never had beer before."

He raises his eyebrows. "You grew up in one of the largest brewing states and you've never had beer before? How is that even possible?"

I sit up tall. "I'm not twenty-one. It's illegal."

He smirks. "It appears as if you're turning over a new leaf, you little rebel."

He pours another glass and offers it to me. I down half the glass before replying. "Apparently, I am."

He holds his mug towards mine. "Shall we toast, rebel?"

I smile. "Do people normally toast with beer?"

He shrugs. "I don't know. But that's not going to stop me. What should we toast to?"

I think about it for a second. "To new friends?"

With an unbelievably sexy grin he asks, "What if I want to explore being more than friends?"

I roll my eyes. "Do you ever give up?"

I find myself staring at his dimples as he replies, "Not when I see something I want."

I sigh and get serious again. "Riley, I could really use a friend right now. I just lost my last surviving parent and moved away from everything I've ever known. I need to focus on school and getting my life together. I don't have room for anything else."

He considers that for a moment with sincere empathy in his big brown eyes. He clinks his glass to mine and says, "To friends, then. I'll be the best damn one you've ever had."

TWO

SOPHOMORE YEAR

DEVYN

I'M OVER AT RILEY'S place watching a basketball game. He decided to live off campus and rented an apartment with his friend, Josh. I mostly hang out here because I'm still stuck in university housing. Thankfully, I got a small single this year that has a private bath so it's not awful but it's really cramped. Rye asked me to take the other bedroom in this place before he considered Josh but I didn't have the budget for it. My brother and I sold our parents' house last year and I only had enough money to get me through all four years of school with dorm housing. I decided that living on campus was the more responsible thing to do. I'd rather not have to get a part time job that could potentially sacrifice my study time and I definitely didn't want to take out student loans if I didn't have to.

"That's BULLSHIT! Get your head out of your ass and put the damn ball in the basket!" Riley yells. "Jesus fucking Christ!"

I give him a cheeky grin. "Aw, what's the matter, Rye? Afraid of losing to a girl *again*?" Riley's a huge Lakers fan. I'm a Blazers girl. Portland is up by twenty points at the bottom of the fourth quarter. The loser has to buy pizza next time. I plan to order an extra-large with the works since he'll be paying.

He pulls me into a playful headlock and yanks on my ponytail. "Watch it, Summers. I know your weaknesses."

I punch his leg. "Ha! I have no weaknesses!"

He maneuvers me so I'm now lying across the couch on my back with my head in his lap. "You think so?"

I lift my chin and stick my tongue out at him. "I *know* so."

He raises his eyebrow and gives me a smile that has made many panties drop. "You think you're so smart, huh?" He lifts his hand into view and slowly lowers it towards my rib cage. Oh heck no, he'd better not!

I widen my eyes. "Riley, don't even think about it!"

He wiggles his fingers. "Don't think about what, Dev? I thought you didn't have any weaknesses? What are you so worried about?"

I try to squirm away but he moves his big body so he's now on top of me, pinning me to the couch. He has both of my hands cuffed above my head with one of his and his other hand is hovering above me threateningly. "Riley, don't you dare!"

"Don't I dare, *what*?" His fingertips brush my ribs and begin to move quickly.

I squeal as he begins his tickle torture. I am so ridiculously ticklish, it's embarrassing. I buck and scream and laugh so hard I'm crying. "STOP! Please stop! You're going to make me pee my pants!"

Josh laughs at us and gets up from the recliner to answer a knock at the door. "Man, don't make her pee. I like that couch."

Riley steps up his pace. "I'll have it cleaned. This is too much fun."

"Aaah! Riley please! STOP! Seriously! I'm about to go all geriatric on you!"

He stops and presses his body into mine holding me in place. He tightens his grip on my hands and says, "Remember that next time you want to talk smack about my team."

His body is stretched over mine and he's staring at my mouth. If I didn't know better, I'd swear he wants to kiss me right now. He shifts slightly and I can feel something hard against my thigh. *Oh my God, is that his—?*

"Riley," a pissy female voice says, "what are you doing?"

Riley jumps off the couch. Oh wow! I can totally see a penis-shaped bulge in his pants! He catches me looking and winks while he adjusts himself. *Winks!* What the heck is going on?

He walks up to the tiny brunette and pulls her in for a kiss. "Hey, Megan. We were just playing around. You remember Devyn, right?"

She crosses her arms over her giant boobs. "Uh huh. How could I forget? What's she doing here?"

I get up from the couch and walk over to the attached kitchen to grab a beer out of the fridge. I hold one out to Rye's flavor of the month as a peace offering. "Megan, do you want a beer?"

Her face twists in distaste. "Ew. I'll have a wine cooler though."

I laugh. She may be kind of bitchy but at least she has a sense of humor. "Ha! Good one."

She glares at me. "What's so funny?"

I twist the top off the bottle and take a swig. "The whole wine cooler joke. It was funny. Like anyone really drinks wine coolers anymore."

Riley clears his throat. "Uh, Dev—"

Megan suddenly turns beet red. "You *bitch*! First, I find you all over my man and then you insult my choice of beverage? What the hell is wrong with you? Why don't you go find a man of your own to hang out with, you little slut?"

Oh, no she didn't! I set my beer on the counter and lunge for her but Josh steps in and holds me back. "*Excuse me?* Who the heck are you calling a slut?" I give her a good once over and take in her low cut top with denim mini skirt. "Have you looked in the mirror lately, Snooki?"

She's clawing at Riley's forearms while he holds her back. "Yeah, I have, and I look good! Which is more than I can say for you. You're never going to get a boyfriend with the whole Amazonian Plain Jane thing you have going on!"

I lunge for her again. "For the record, I already *have* a boyfriend! I swear to God, Riley, if you don't get her out of here, I'm going to punch her in the throat."

"Dude, this is so hot!" Josh says.

Riley tightens his grip on her. "Megan, calm the fuck down. Devyn is going to be here whether you like it or not. Do I need to ask you to leave or are you going to behave?"

She breaks away from his hold and lets out a big huff. "Fine."

Josh looks at me. "You good, baby girl?"

He releases his hold on me when I nod. "I'll be good."

Riley leads Megan towards the couch. "C'mon, babe, let's watch the rest of the game."

She trails her finger down his chest and hooks it under his waistband. "I don't want to watch basketball."

"It certainly doesn't compare to a day at the mall," I mutter.

Megan glares at me and leans into Riley, whispering in his ear.

Riley smiles at whatever she's saying. "Uh, if you guys

need me I'll be in my room. But really, don't knock unless the building is on fire."

With that, Megan jumps on his back like a monkey and he carries her off to his bedroom, slamming the door behind them.

I roll my eyes. "Ugh, what does he see in that girl? She's such a wench."

Josh shrugs. "Maybe. But from what I hear, her rack is to die for and she has a mouth like a Hoover."

I make a puking gesture. "Gross, Josh! Way too much information!"

He laughs and grabs a bottle of whiskey from the cabinet. "C'mon, baby girl, let's watch the end of the game and get sloppy drunk. If you're lucky, I might get so wasted I'll let you take advantage of my hot body."

I nudge his shoulder as I join him on the couch. "A girl can only hope."

Moaning filters out through Riley's bedroom. I glare at the closed door and grab the TV remote to increase the volume.

Josh looks at the door, then back to me and hands me the bottle of Jack with a strange expression on his face. "Here, darlin', you look like you could use this."

I grab the bottle from him and take a giant swig. Wiping my hand across my face I say, "Thanks, Josh."

RILEY

THE SMELL OF COFFEE wakes me up. I walk into the living room and see a makeshift bed on the couch. I glance over to the attached kitchen and find Devyn standing in front of the coffee maker tapping her fingers on the counter. I can't help but check out the mile long legs peeking out of the oversized t-shirt that she's wearing. I frown as I come closer when I notice that it's Josh's favorite shirt. We make eye contact as I reach over her head to grab two mugs out of the cabinet.

I set them in front of the pot. "Here ya go."

She pours some coffee into both mugs. "Thanks."

We stand there in companionable silence for a minute while Devyn loads her cup with milk and sugar. She closes her eyes and moans upon taking her first sip. My dick jumps towards the sound.

I shift a little to conceal my burgeoning hard-on. "Hey, I'm sorry about the thing with Megan last night. She gets a little crazy when she feels threatened."

She shrugs. "It's fine."

Before I can argue, Josh steps out of his bedroom and joins us in the kitchen. He ruffles Devyn's hair and takes a sip from her mug. "How's my favorite girl this morning?"

She takes her mug back from him and continues drinking like it's no big deal they're swapping spit right now. What the fuck? When did they get so cozy?

"Tired," she says. "Your couch sucks. I slept like crap."

He winks at her. "Hey, you were the one who refused my big, comfy bed. Don't say I didn't offer."

"Ah, but here's the problem with that: You were *in* said big, comfy bed and I didn't feel like fighting off your drunken advances all night."

Josh laughs. "Hey, you were just as smashed as I was so for all I know, *I* would've been fighting off *your* drunken advances all night."

Devyn rolls her eyes. "Yeah, in your dreams, pig."

Josh laughs harder this time, ruffles her hair again, and walks back into his room without another word. Seriously, what the hell is going on with these two? Josh has always been flirty with her but this feels different. Did something happen between them last night?

"What was that about?" I growl.

She raises her eyebrows. "What was *what* about?"

I fling my hand towards Josh's room. "You and Josh. Since when are you two so touchy feely sharing coffee? Do you think your boyfriend would appreciate that?"

She rolls her eyes. "Oh geez, Riley. You're making a big deal out of nothing. You and I normally share the same *bed* when I stay over and Brian's never had a problem with it. He knows we're just friends and he trusts me."

I cross my arms over my chest. "Well, I don't like it. Josh is different."

She narrows her eyes at me. "And why's that?"

We're interrupted again when Megan steps out of my bedroom. She looks thoroughly fucked but she clearly touched up her hair and makeup before coming out here. I look back towards Devyn and can't help but appreciate how good she always looks first thing in the morning with no makeup, bed head, and a wrinkled tee.

Megan glares at Devyn. "What are you still doing here?"

Devyn takes another sip. "I stayed the night. I had too much to drink last night to walk back to the dorms and Josh was in no condition to drive me."

Megan puts her hand on her hip and looks at me. "Does this happen often?"

I shrug. "Sometimes." I intentionally leave out the part about Devyn usually sleeping in my room.

Devyn smirks when she sees the fire in Megan's eyes. I can't help but mirror her expression.

Megan saunters over to me, pulls my head down and kisses me. Hard. With a shit load of tongue. "I have to get going to Psych class. Thanks for the incredible night, baby. I think I'll be walking funny for a week." She winks as she walks out the door.

Devyn rolls her eyes again. "Incredible night, huh?"

I rub my neck, totally embarrassed by Megan's over the top territorial behavior. I guess it's time to end things with her. "Uh...I guess."

Devyn laughs and says, "Well, Megan certainly seems to think so."

"Yeah, Megan is actually starting to get on my nerves so I think I'm going to cut her loose."

"Does she know that?"

I shrug. "She knew this wasn't going anywhere when she signed up. We're just having fun; she'll be fine."

"Fun?" Devyn asks. "Is that what you call it?"

"Yeah, fun. That's all it ever is. These girls aren't interested in getting to know me. They want one thing from me and I'm okay with that."

"Don't you get tired of it, Rye? Don't you want a real connection with someone?"

I smile. "That's what I have you for."

Devyn bites her lip, looking frustrated, but for the life of me, I can't figure out why. "Yeah, I guess you're right." As she picks up her folded clothes and heads for the bathroom she adds, "I have to get going too. I'm supposed to meet Brian at ten o'clock."

I keep talking to her through the door. "What are you guys up to this morning?"

"We're just going to grab some coffee and head to the library."

"Are you sure he's okay with you staying here all the time?" I ask. "If I were him, I don't think I would be."

She comes out of the bathroom wearing her clothes from last night. "I swear. We've talked about it quite a few times.

He says he's secure enough in our relationship and if I say we're just friends, he trusts me implicitly."

"And why is it that we're just friends again?" I try keeping my tone light to suggest that I'm joking, but I'm really not. We haven't visited the subject since we first met, but last night I almost kissed her while we were playing around on the couch. I don't know what came over me, but I know she sensed it, and I have a sneaking suspicion she might have actually kissed me back.

She pokes me in the chest with her index finger. "Because you, my friend, are a total slut."

I laugh. "Oh, yeah, that's right. Why do I keep forgetting that?"

Devyn shakes her head. "I have no idea. Lucky you have me around to keep reminding you, right?"

"Right," I agree halfheartedly.

THREE

JUNIOR YEAR

DEVYN

EVERY YEAR, I COME back home the week before fall semester begins to visit my parents' graves. This year, Riley insisted on making the trip with me. We step through the wrought iron gates of Rogue Valley Cemetery and make our way over to an old oak tree. A light breeze floats through the air carrying the scents of nearby rose bushes and an impending storm.

I kneel down and lovingly trace the dates on the simple, flat stones marking their graves. My mom was only thirty-eight when she died and my dad was forty-six. They both had so much life to live but God had other plans for them, I guess. "Hi, Mom and Dad."

Riley lowers himself to the ground and takes my hand, silently urging me to continue.

I nod towards Rye. "This is Riley. My friend from school that I was telling you about." I look into his eyes and smile. "My best friend. We're about to start our third year of college. I can't believe we're already halfway done. Before you know it, I'll be taking the marketing world by storm with my brilliant ad campaigns and Riley will be a jet designer extraordinaire."

Riley smiles and squeezes my hand. "You know it."

I look back towards their graves and sniff back a tear. "I miss you both so much every day. I miss this town. I know you wanted me to follow in your footsteps and attend SOU but I just couldn't be here every day, being reminded of everything that I've lost. I hope you're proud of me, even if I am a Duck now." I look back at Riley. "I have to believe that's what I was meant to be. I wouldn't have Riley if I wasn't at U of O. I don't know if I could've made it through the past two years without him."

Riley pulls me into a side hug and kisses the top of my head. "Do you mind if I say something?"

I wrap my arm around his torso and hug him tighter. "Not at all."

He clears his throat. "Hi, Mr. and Mrs. Summers. I know we haven't officially met, but Devyn's told me a lot about you. You raised the most incredible person I know and I wanted to thank you for bringing her into this world. I don't know what I'd do without her and I promise I'll take care of her. Hell, I'm even letting her drag me to a play tonight. That should tell you how invested I am in our girl here. I don't willingly watch men in tights spit all over each other for just anyone."

My sobs fall away as my laughter takes over. I love that he can cheer me up so easily. No one has ever been able to do so like he can. "Thank you, Rye."

He squeezes me into him. "Cometh, milady. Let's go see if you can change my mind about this festival."

. . .

RILEY

FROM FEBRUARY THROUGH OCTOBER, the town of Ashland is taken over by the Oregon Shakespeare Festival. They boast three theaters, rotating eleven plays throughout each season. While they also offer non-Shakespeare works, my mom would never consider attending anything that wasn't written by the festival's namesake himself. I've never been much of a fan, but Devyn apparently shares the same passion for good ol' William.

We're seeing Antony and Cleopatra tonight in the outdoor Elizabethan theater. Our seats are in the balcony so we have a perfect view of the pink and purple sky as the sun sets behind the mountains. I'm honestly not paying much consideration to the actors; I'm much more interested in the woman beside me. Every once in a while, Devyn looks over and catches me staring at her. She simply smiles and returns her eyes to the stage. I don't think she has any clue that I'm studying her so closely. She watches with rapt attention for hours as Mark Antony repeatedly neglects his soldierly duties after being beguiled by the Queen of Egypt. Blah, blah, blah, battles are waged. Blah, blah, blah, they both die in the end. Typical tragedy.

The full gamut of emotions runs over her face as she sits there, enraptured by the story. I'm seeing another side of her tonight. She's normally just one of the guys—albeit, in a hot chick's body, but still one of the guys. She's totally into sports, hanging out, drinking beer, eating pizza, shooting pool...you know, normal dude stuff. Right now, I'm seeing the cultured, sophisticated, feminine person that lies beneath the surface. Trust me, my dick is aware of her womanly parts *at all times*, especially when she's wearing a dress like she is tonight, but

I've never seen her in this light before today. I'm itching to find out more about *this* Devyn.

I realize the play is over as Devyn stands. "Riley, are you coming?"

I get out of my seat and take the hand she is offering. We filter out of the theater and begin walking around the town square. She hasn't pulled her hand away yet and I'm not complaining.

"Care to commemorate your visit to our festival?"

Devyn stops mid-stride as the street vendor asks his question. "I'm sorry, were you talking to us?"

The robust man in full costume holds up his camera. "Milady, I'd be honored to take a picture of such a lovely couple." He gestures to the wooden kiosk that holds several mementos available for purchase. "Perhaps you'd like to take home a framed photo? We also offer magnets and key chains if you'd like something smaller."

She blushes. "Oh, right. Um…we aren't a couple. We're just friends."

The vendor looks at our joined hands. "My apologies for the error, milady. Perhaps a photo between *friends*, then?"

She follows his gaze and pulls out of my grip. "Oh, uh… no, thank you."

I awkwardly put my hands in my pockets as we start walking again. "You feel like walking for a while before we head back to the hotel?"

"Sure." She holds out her hand and smiles. "Screw it. Who said friends can't hold hands?"

I smirk as I take my hand out of my pocket and link our fingers together. "Not me."

She squeezes my fingers. "Me neither."

As we stroll through a large park I ask, "So, what did you think of the play?"

Her face lights up. "Oh, I loved it! I think they did such a good job! I've never seen that particular one before. It was beautiful...I think Cleopatra is definitely one of Shakespeare's more complex characters. You feel empathy for her one minute, but then hate her in the next. Ya know? What did *you* think? Was the festival better than you remembered?"

I pull her arm and jerk her into my body. "No offense to my mom, but the company was definitely better this time around."

She tucks her chin. We're so close that I can feel the rapid beat of her heart. Her breath catches when her tits brush against my chest. I'm not positive, but I think I see her nipples poking out. Fuck me, but my dick just became rock hard thinking about it. We stand facing each other, chest to chest, just breathing without a word. *Oh fuck it,* I think before taking one step closer so she can feel the evidence of how she affects me.

Devyn gasps and tilts her face up. "Riley, what are—"

I put my index finger on her lips to silence her protest. "Shhh. I just need to see something."

I lean down slowly towards her mouth. I don't know why I'm about to cross this line after two years of a strictly platonic—okay, *mostly* platonic—relationship, but I can't seem to stop myself. She holds herself completely still waiting for me to make my move. I need to know if she's feeling what I'm feeling. I don't even know how to articulate exactly *what* I'm feeling right now, but it's definitely something.

She turns her face away right before our lips touch. "It's starting to rain."

I pull back and shake my head to clear the fog. "Huh?"

She looks up towards the sky and wipes a raindrop off her forehead. "The storm is rolling in. We'd better start walking back before it gets too bad."

"Right," I say.

We're a block away from my truck when the sky opens

up. We start running through the downpour. Devyn squeals as the drops become heavier and heavier. Suddenly she stops and turns around to face me. She gets this big smile on her face, holds her arms out wide and spins in circles repeatedly. She tilts her face up to the sky as she twirls and laughs.

"What's so funny?"

"This rain is ridiculous! We're soaked! I figured there's no point in running from it so why not enjoy it?" She begins turning in circles again, laughing like a loon. She's fucking gorgeous.

Without any further thought, I advance upon her and back her into the side of my truck. Surprise has made her laughter fall silent immediately. I can see the wheels turning in her mind trying to process what's happening. She pulls out of my hold and takes three steps to the side. "Riley, what are you doing?"

Okay, I'm trying not to be a dick here but that's kind of hard —pun intended—to do when her pink sundress is soaking wet and plastered to her body. The streetlight above is shining brightly so I can clearly see *every* curve on her body. She's wearing a lacy bra and I swear to God her nipples are taunting me saying, "Touch me! Suck me! Lick me!"

She crosses her arms over her chest. "Riley! Stop staring at my boobs!"

I throw my hands up in frustration. "Tell your boobs to stop staring at my eyes!"

She looks down and notices how transparent her dress is. "Oh my God, I might as well be naked! I can't believe this is happening right now." She puts her hand on the passenger door. "Can we please just go?"

I pull my keys out of my pocket and hit the button to unlock the door. She climbs in before I have a chance to open it for her. I walk around to the other side and get behind the wheel. I turn the ignition and crank the heat.

She's holding her hands against the vent as I fumble behind me looking for the sweatshirt I had in the backseat. I finally find it and hold it out towards her.

She grabs it and starts pulling it around her shoulders. After zipping it up to the neck she says, "Thanks."

"No prob." I put the truck into gear and pull onto the road. "Devyn, I don't know what just almost happened back there, but I think we need to talk about it."

She groans. "Can we please just forget it ever happened?"

I look over towards her and raise my eyebrows. "Really? Is that what you really want?"

She sighs. "Yeah, I do. It was stupid."

I frown. "Stupid?"

She pushes her wet hair out of her face. "Yeah, completely stupid. I was emotional from earlier, and well, you're a dude. My dress is totally see-through and you reacted like any straight guy would. It's no big deal."

I'm about to point out that I almost kissed her *before* her dress was clinging to her body but she gives me this pleading look as if she's begging me to drop it. "You're probably right. I was thinking with my other head for a second there. Sorry about that. It's totally no big deal." I laugh to emphasize the breeziness of my statement.

She laughs with me. "Right."

FOUR

SENIOR YEAR

DEVYN

I GULP NERVOUSLY. "OKAY, here's the thing. I'm a virgin. And you need to relieve me of that."

Riley sprays beer from his mouth all over the table. "The fuck you say?"

I steel my nerves and grab a napkin to start wiping up the mess he made. "We're graduating next week. I can't move to Portland, officially starting my adult life, without having had sex."

Riley gapes at me, speechless. "How in the hell are you still a virgin? You're twenty-two! More importantly, how the fuck have I not known that when we've been together practically every day for the past four years?"

I sigh, dreading this part of the conversation that I inevitably knew was coming. "Look, I know I'm not your type, but I figured since you've screwed practically every vagina in Eugene since freshman year you wouldn't be so opposed to throwing me a bone. It's not a big deal. I'm not asking you to marry me. Or even date me. I just want one night of sex from someone who knows what they're doing, so I can finally understand what the big deal is. You're the only one I trust, Rye." I grab his hand and look at him pleadingly. "I figured we could do it this weekend when you help me move."

RILEY

I TAKE A LONG pull from my bottle. Then another. And another. I can't believe what's happening right now. How can the hottest girl I've ever known be a virgin? And what the fuck did she mean she wasn't my type? She's EVERY guy's type. Has she been avoiding mirrors her entire life? She has legs that go on for miles, perfectly rounded tits, and an ass that was made to be grabbed. All of that with the face of an angel. A Victoria's Secret angel. Even if she didn't look like a supermodel, her personality would win over any guy with half a brain. She's perfectly happy hanging out at The Duck Pond for hours watching a game. She couldn't care less about shopping, or getting her nails done, or all that other girly shit. She's definitely all woman and sexy as hell, but it's effortless for her.

Okay, so maybe she has no clue that almost every dude at U of O has the hots for her, but never in a million years would I have expected this. I'd be all up in that shit if she hadn't friend-zoned me on the first day we met. Initially, I wasn't going to give up, but the more I got to know her, the more I didn't want to risk our friendship by pushing for more. We had a few near slips over the years, but I managed to keep it in my pants which for me, is a pretty big feat. And now she's asking me for it? Am I dreaming?

How in the hell is she still a virgin? She's dated guys throughout school. Hasn't she? I think for a minute. Yeah, she has! There's been at least a handful that I can think of. Then there was that one guy from sophomore year that hung around for a while. What was his name again? Oh yeah, Brian!

"What about Brian?" I ask. "You dated him for like six months."

Devyn rolls her eyes. "Please, Rye, Brian is a walking stereotype! I didn't see it at the time, but I was totally his cover girlfriend until he was ready to come out of the closet. He broke up with me for someone named Michael, for Christ's sake! And I'm going to their wedding next month! How could you have missed that?"

What? "Shit, I thought you said *Michelle*." I start rubbing the back of my neck. "Now that you mention it though, it was pretty obvious. Damn! How did I miss that?"

Devyn laughs. "No clue...you were probably too consumed with picking out the lucky brunette of the month."

I scowl. "Hey, I'm not that bad!"

Devyn laughs even harder. "Oh, please! You are such a man whore! But that's okay given the circumstances. I know you're the right person for this. I don't want to lose my V-card to just anyone. I've messed around with guys before but I always thought that final moment should be with someone that I was in love with. Since that hasn't happened, I'm okay with it being someone that I trust. You're the only guy who fits that description for me, Rye. And like I said earlier, your bedroom skills are legendary. I want my first time to be good. I want it to be with you. Besides, you kinda owe me."

I smile at her comment about my skills. I can't help myself. I do know my way around a woman's body. And I know that women talk. I count on it, actually, which is why I haven't had to ask anyone out in years. They all come on to me because they hear the rumors and want to see firsthand if they're true. And I'm usually more than happy to oblige. I never really cared that they didn't stick around long enough to get to know me. Devyn knew the real me and that was good enough. All those other women thought I was just a body. Devyn knows my mind. Now that I think about it, she's the only woman not related to me who knows that I'm a certified genius, not the dumb jock they all assumed. Hell, I'm graduating with high honors next week and headed to Boston for my Master's in Aerospace Engineering. The average Joe can't claim that.

I start to seriously consider her proposal. Can I do this? Can I worship her glorious body and, let's be honest here, probably ruin her for any guy that would come after me, and then pretend it never happened? Go back to being just friends? If we weren't about to move three thousand miles away from each other, I'd say it was impossible. As it stands, it seems quite possible. Maybe it's just my dick talking, but this idea of hers sounds better and better with each passing second. Wait a minute…did she just say I owe her?

"Owe you for what?"

She rolls her eyes. "Part of the reason I'm in this predicament is because I've spent almost every day over the past four years with you. Every guy I've liked, besides Brian, backed off once they found out about you. I never got past a few dates with any of them. They all thought we were an item or something. No one ever believed me when I said we were just friends."

Okay, so *maybe* I had a word or two with these guys. And *maybe* I led them to believe that Devyn was off limits. I'm pleading the fifth.

"So to be clear, you want me to have sex with you. For one night and one night only. No strings attached, no emotions, just sex so you can turn in your V-card, as you call it. Afterwards, we pretend as if it never happened and go back to normal?"

Devyn nods and chews her bottom lip.

"I need to hear the words, Dev."

She holds her chin up. "Yes. Just sex. No strings. Afterwards, best buds like always. Do we have a deal?"

I smile bigger than I probably ever have before. "Deal."

FIVE

DEVYN

WE MAKE THE THREE hour drive north to Portland along Interstate-5. I'm super nervous about this weekend but Riley hasn't brought it up so I can't seem to either. Did he change his mind? God, I hope not. I'm starting a highly sought after paid internship next month at a huge marketing firm. The owner of the agency and the founder of Nike were both U of O alums. They open one slot every year for a graduating student. I worked my butt off creating mock ups for Nike's new children's line. Out of over three hundred applicants, they picked me. Now for the next year of my life, I get to learn from some of the best in the industry. I feel like everything is falling into place perfectly according to plan. Everything except my love life, anyway. And I'm honestly okay with that—I wouldn't have time for a relationship right now. But let's face it. Sex sells. It's *huge* in the marketing world and I can pretend all day long but I know I'll never truly get it until I experience it for myself. I know Riley is the right person to help me with my little dilemma. I don't know what I'm going to do if he backs out.

"Why are you fidgeting so much over there?" Riley asks.

I look down and notice that I'm wringing my hands incessantly. I decide to bite the bullet and talk about the elephant in the room. Or the car, rather.

"Did you change your mind?" I ask.

"About what? Helping you move? It's a little late now, don't ya think, considering we're only a few minutes outside of town?"

Oh no! Maybe he forgot about our deal! That's even worse than him changing his mind. I clear my throat. "No... um, not about helping me move. Which I appreciate very much, if I haven't mentioned that already. About...the other thing."

He raises one eyebrow and smirks. "The other thing?"

I throw my hands up in exasperation, now knowing he's just screwing with me. "Oh God, Riley! Are you really going to make me say it? The deal we made...to you know, have sex."

He gives me that devastating smile that showcases his dimples. "Oh, *the deal*. No, I definitely haven't changed my mind about *that*."

I sink into my chair, trying to hide my discomfort. "Oh. Good."

He grabs my hand and squeezes. "Baby, I promise to make it *much* better than good."

I roll my eyes, pulling my hand away. "Gah! How many women have you said that to?" He manages to look a little embarrassed. "Don't forget who you're talking to, Rye. I've seen too many women fall victim to that panty-melting grin and your charming ways. That crap doesn't work on me."

Not really, anyway.

His smile gets even bigger. "You think my smile melts panties, huh?"

I try to hide my grin but fail miserably. "You know what I mean. Just don't try to dress this up into something it's not. Okay? After we unload the car, you and I will have sex real quick, and then it'll be back to the same ol' same ol'. We can grab some burgers and beer afterwards. It's no big deal. Really."

He shakes his head. "Nuh uh. I didn't agree to that. If we do this, Devyn, we do it on my terms."

"What's that supposed to mean?"

"It means," he replies as he pulls off the freeway leading us into the heart of Portland's Pearl District, "that if we do this...no, scratch that. *When* we do this, I'm in charge. And '*real quick*', ain't gonna happen, sweetheart."

"Domineering much? I didn't say I wanted to explore S&M."

His eyes glitter with...lust? No, that can't be right. "I wasn't talking about anything kinky." He wiggles his eyebrows. "Well, nothing *too* kinky. What I'm trying to say is that this will *not* be a wham, bam, thank you ma'am sort of thing. No way. If that's what you want, I'm out."

Wait...what? "Huh? I'm confused."

He pulls into the parking garage beneath my new apartment building. Thankfully he's been here once before when I signed the lease so I don't have to direct him with my befuddled brain. Grabbing my hand again he says, "Devyn, I'm not going to be an asshole who just takes pleasure for himself. This is your first time. You said yourself you wanted it to feel good which is partly why you chose me. I'm going to make sure that happens. That's not going to be possible unless you're loosened up beforehand."

"Okay...and how do we accomplish that?"

He pulls into a spot near the elevator and puts the car in park. "You just leave that to me, baby."

Call the panty fire department...*there's that grin again*!

RILEY

"YOU JUST LEAVE THAT to me, baby." Okay, I know that was a cheesy line but if the blush staining her cheeks is any indication...I'd say I'm peaking her interest. But damn, does she really think so little of me that she actually believes I'd rid her of her pesky virginity and just walk away? The last time I was with a virgin was when I *was* a virgin, but the one thing I learned from that flop is that it is not comfortable when a woman loses hers. I was a sixteen-year-old punk back then who had no idea what he was doing. I still harbor guilt for not knowing beforehand that a woman needs to be well prepared for sex, especially if she's never done it before.

I'm going to make damn sure I don't repeat that mistake again. Devyn is going to be seduced. And not in a creepy, take advantage kind of way. I mean she's going to be wined and dined, and when the time comes to remove our clothes, she will be worshipped. I will make her body feel so good by the time we're done that she will never be able to have sex again without comparing it to our time together. Okay, so technically I'll be walking away afterwards since I'm moving to Boston next week, but it's not like we won't talk or visit each other as often as possible. She'll continue being my best friend only she'll know what I looked like naked once upon a time. See? Totally different.

"Seriously, how do we accomplish that?" she insists. "I'm a planner; you know this. My brain doesn't like spontaneity."

I laugh. She really is a Type A personality but it's

adorable as hell. "Well, too bad. I made the plans for this weekend, and your brain is just going to have to handle going with the flow."

"You made *plans*?"

I narrow my eyes at her. "Well, you don't have to sound so shocked."

She starts wringing her hands again. "Quite frankly, I am."

"Why?"

"Well, *you're* the one doing *me* a favor here. Why would you need to plan anything extra?"

I roll my eyes. "Having sex with you won't exactly be a hardship, Dev. Have you looked in a mirror lately?"

There goes the blush again. "You think I'm pretty?"

"Are you fucking kidding me?" I scoff in disbelief. "You're easily the hottest chick I know."

"But…"

"But what?" I press.

"But, you normally date brunettes. Petite, perky brunettes."

"So?"

"So? Well, I'm blonde for one. And gangly. And certainly nowhere near perky."

Wow, how the hell did she ever develop this complex? Time to start the seduction and set the record straight. Grabbing her hand, I bring her index finger to my lips. "For one, who gives a fuck what color your hair is?" Kiss. "All I care about is that it's long enough to wrap around my fist when I'm fucking you senseless. Two," I grab the next finger and briefly pull the tip into my mouth. "You're *tall*, not gangly. I'm fairly certain every dude you've ever met has imagined those long legs wrapped around his hips… or better yet, hanging over his shoulders while he's tasting you." Loving the darkened blush on her cheeks I add, "I certainly know I have more than once."

Oh, yes, she's definitely getting warmed up now; the flush has spread across her collarbone. Not being strong enough to resist, I lean over and nip that sweet spot where her neck meets her shoulder and grin when I feel her shiver. Good to know she's not as immune as she claims. "And three," I'm kissing up her neck now... "Perky is annoying. Nobody is naturally perky all the time which means those girls that I date are fake. You're *real*, Devyn. What you see is what you get and there is *nothing* sexier than a woman who's not afraid to be herself."

While I'm kissing her jawbone she pants, "Riley, what are you doing?"

I grin against her cheek. "I'm seducing you."

She gasps. "Why?" She chuckles a little in an effort, I think, to conceal her obvious nervousness. "I'm a sure thing."

I grab her face with both hands, forcing her to look at me. "Because you *deserve* to be seduced. And I'm talking full-scale seduction here. Never settle for anything less, Devyn. Before we do this, you have to promise me that. That you will *never* settle."

Her eyes bulge slightly. "What did you just say?"

"Promise me that you'll never settle, Devyn. Never sell yourself short and settle for someone out of comfort or obligation. Make sure that when you do settle down one day it's with someone who knows your worth and makes you *feel* everything you're supposed to feel with the person you spend the rest of your life with."

"I promise," she whispers.

SIX

RILEY

AFTER CARRYING SOME STUFF upstairs, I throw a backpack towards the floor by Devyn's feet. "Pack anything you'll need into the morning."

"We're not staying here?" she asks.

I look around her studio apartment. Her *empty* apartment with the exception of the few boxes we brought with us. "Dev, the furniture isn't being delivered until tomorrow. Were you planning to sleep on the floor?"

She bites her bottom lip. "I honestly didn't think about it. I guess I've had a lot on my mind."

I smile. "Good thing I've made some plans, isn't it?" I nod towards the bag. "Hurry up so we can make it to the Heathman in time for happy hour."

"Like Ana and Christian's Heathman?"

"Who the fuck are they?"

"Duh, Riley. *Ana* and *Christian*. From Fifty Shades? The

Heathman is where they first kiss. It has quite a bit of significance in the book."

I roll my eyes. "First of all, you really need to quit reading those novels. Secondly, they have a great happy hour menu and it's close to our next item on the agenda. Purely coincidental."

"What's the next item on the agenda?"

"Nice try. You'll just have to wait and see."

After she packs her bag, we take the streetcar into the heart of downtown Portland. We walk along the sidewalks until we round a corner and land directly in front of the Heathman Hotel. We're seated by a window in the bar and order some drinks with appetizers. Devyn nurses her Jack and Seven while we eat and make small talk. Out of nowhere, she gets a full body shiver that's pretty hard to ignore.

"You cold?" I ask.

"What? Oh, uh…no. I just can't believe I'm actually sitting in *the* Heathman right now."

I lift an eyebrow. "The book again?"

"Uh, yeah!"

"Isn't Fifty Shades that bondage book? You starting to change your mind about trying a little S&M?"

Devyn's jaw drops. "No! And it is *so* much more than that! It's a beautiful love story. She's the healing balm for his shattered soul!"

I shake my head in disbelief. "Yeah, I'm sure the *love story* is why you enjoy it so much."

She narrows her eyes at me. "Why else would I like it?"

"Oh, I don't know…the dirty, dirty fucking maybe?"

"Whatever," she huffs, blushing profusely.

"Why are you blushing, Devyn? Because I'm talking about fucking?"

"No!" she denies.

"Since when are you so nervous around me?" I know she's getting turned on thinking about her lady porn and I'm going to milk this as much as possible.

She squirms in her seat. "I'm not nervous."

I laugh. "Liar. Don't forget who *you're* with."

She crosses her arms over her chest, pushing her tits up for my viewing pleasure, and sticks out her tongue. "Whatever."

I look at my watch and signal for the waitress to settle our tab. "Save that tongue for later. And hurry up and finish your drink. We have to get to our next destination."

Her blush deepens. "And where was that again?"

"I'm not going to slip, Devyn, so quit trying to get it out of me." I sign the receipt and stand up to offer my hand. "C'mon, let's go.

DEVYN

WE WALK ONLY A couple blocks and end up at Pioneer Courthouse Square, also known as Portland's living room. It spans an entire city block in the heart of downtown. The center of the square is arranged like an amphitheater where a semicircle of approximately two dozen steps serves as seating. On the west side, there's a small visitor's center framed by a cascading waterfall with a coffee shop sitting up above. The entire thing is paved by red bricks, many of which are inscribed with people's names .

There's a large projector screen set up in the corner. We make our way through the crowd and find an open spot on the steps. Riley reaches into the bag he's carrying and pulls out a woolen blanket, spreading it over our legs as we sit down.

It's obvious there will be a film showing so I ask, "What's playing tonight?"

He smiles. "*Anchorman.*"

I slam my open hand into his chest excitedly. "No way!" *Anchorman* is one of my all-time favorite movies. Riley reaches into his bag and pulls out two mini bottles of scotch. I grin big and recite one of my favorite quotes from the movie using my best Ron Burgundy impression. "*I love scotch! I love scotch! Scotchy scotch scotch. Here it goes down, down into my belly.*"

I chug the bottle and belch afterwards, slamming my palm over my mouth in embarrassment.

Riley laughs. "Sexy, Dev."

As we watch the film, the temperatures drop. I start rubbing my arms to get warm.

Riley stands and says, "I'll be right back."

I watch as he walks over to the opposite corner and steps inside Starbucks. He returns a few minutes later with two large cups of hot chocolate. He reaches into his bag again and pulls out two airline bottles of marshmallow vodka. I had no idea such a thing existed!

"We're drinking grown up hot chocolate tonight," he explains.

He pops both of our lids, which conveniently have some room left in the cup and pours the vodka, bringing the chocolatey liquid right to the rim.

I take my first sip and moan. "Oh my God, this is pure heaven." I continue drinking until my cup runs dry. I feel slightly buzzed and can't stop thinking how wonderful tonight has been so far.

When Riley puts his arm around my shoulder, I actually start feeling like this is the most perfect date imaginable. I have to constantly remind myself that this isn't a date; this is Riley. I snuggle into him anyway and he rests his chin on the top of my head. We watch the rest of the movie in the same position.

SEVEN

RILEY

I KNOW I SHOULDN'T be holding her like this but she smells so damn good. Like birthday cake...or maybe sugar cookies, or donuts. Whatever it is, I want to fucking devour her. While the credits roll, she tilts her chin up to look at me and gives me a blinding ear to ear grin. I'm taken aback by how beautiful she is. I can't remember ever seeing her smile this big. Without thinking, I lean down until my lips are brushing against hers. She gasps in surprise which gives me the perfect opportunity to slip my tongue into her mouth. She responds instantly by raking her fingers through my hair and deepening the kiss.

Devyn moans into my mouth, giving me the green light to pull her onto me so she's now straddling my lap. She tastes so fucking sweet I could do this all night. She's grinding her body into mine with reckless abandon. It's like she's starving for me as much as I am for her. Right when my fingers brush the underside of her breast someone whistles and yells, "Get a room!"

I clear my throat, reminded that we're out in public. Devyn quickly scoots off my lap and starts picking up our belongings. She starts fumbling with the blanket, trying to fold it but she drops it three times. I frown when I notice that she won't make eye contact with me.

"Devyn." She ignores me, and picks up the blanket again. I grab her hands, stilling her movement. "Devyn, look at me."

After a few seconds of looking anywhere *but* at me, she lifts her chin and hesitantly meets my eyes. "What is this, Riley?"

I'm confused. "What is *what?*"

She throws her arms out, gesturing to our surroundings. "*This*! All of this! Happy hour at the Heathman? And don't even try claiming it was a coincidence again when you know how much I love those books. Then following it up with one of my favorite movies while snuggling under a blanket? And the hot chocolate? You know how much I love hot chocolate on chilly nights and you took it a step further by spiking it with the most delicious creation I've ever tasted! Why are you doing all of this? These are all very date-like activities. Like, *best date ever* activities!"

"Your point being?"

"This isn't a date, Riley!" she shouts, garnering the attention of some bystanders.

I usher her to some rushing water nearby to drown out our conversation. "Why *isn't* this a date? Especially considering the fact that you want this night to end with a *very good date*-like activity."

She huffs and sits down on the steps. "It *can't* be a date. Dates open the door to possibilities. Possibilities that you and I don't have."

I sit down next to her and grab her hand. "Dev, I know that. *You* know that. I'm just trying to give you a night that you'll remember, okay? Yeah, I had the home court advantage when I was planning it because I know you so well." I grin. "Like I said earlier, you should *never* settle. I just don't want you to look back on this night years from now and feel like you settled. That's all this is. I promise."

She offers me a small smile. "Really?"

I nod my head. "Really."

DEVYN

OH MY GOD, I am thrown way off balance from that kiss! I always knew Riley and I had chemistry but it was never this explosive before. I got a little taste in my car earlier but this is different. That kiss was freaking volcanic! Riley offers his hand which I accept after only a brief hesitation. As he starts leading me across the square I ask, "What now?"

He points to the tall white building on the corner. "Look carefully up on top of that building. Do you see those people looking over the ledge?"

"Yeah. What's up there?"

"It's a restaurant," he replies. "On the roof, anyway. The space in between that and Macy's is a hotel. I figured we could get some dessert and maybe a nightcap before heading downstairs to our room."

"Oh." I stare at the imposing structure. I started to feel warm as soon as he mentioned *our* hotel room. I don't know why I'm acting this way; Riley and I have shared a bed *many* times over the years. But there was always the knowledge that nothing physical would ever happen back then. Now? Not so much.

He grins. "That okay?"

I clear my throat. "What? Um, yeah…of course it's okay."

He increases his stride, towing me behind. "Then let's go."

EIGHT

DEVYN

WE WALK INTO THE lobby of the hotel up to the check-in desk. I stare at the lighted mural behind the counter as Riley tells the clerk we have reservations. He hands her his credit card, signs something, and pockets two keycards.

"Would you like me to have someone take your bags up for you, sir?" she asks.

Riley looks over his shoulder and winks at me. "Yeah, that'd be great. We're going to head upstairs for a nightcap."

"Very well, sir. Please let us know if you need anything. Enjoy your stay."

He leads me to an elevator that takes us up to the rooftop lounge. The hostess seats us at one of the white couches in the open-air balcony. She hands us our menus as Riley orders two shots of Fireball.

When the hostess leaves, I look around. "This place is nice." The city view is lost on me because I'm not really paying attention to our surroundings. I can't stop thinking about the keys in his pocket. The ones that lead to our hotel room. The room where we're going to have sex. After we leave here. Oh God.

"It is," he agrees while looking at the menu. "Do you want to share the tempura banana split?"

I quickly glance at my menu. "Yeah, that sounds good."

Our waiter arrives with our drinks and takes our order. We drink our shots and make small talk until our dessert arrives. My mouth waters as I stare at the plate in front of us. Fried bananas are topped with a cherry compote, peanut brittle ice cream, and caramel sauce.

I lick my lips. "Yum."

Riley is staring at my mouth. "My thoughts exactly." I reach for my silverware but he stops me and says, "Here. Allow me."

"Uh…okay."

He grabs a spoon and dips it into the ice cream. He watches carefully as he brings the bite to my mouth, gulping audibly as I close my lips over the utensil. "Good?"

I swallow. "Yes, very. Are you going to try it?"

"Oh, I really, really want to." He hasn't taken his eyes off of me.

"Well, why don't you—"

I'm silenced when his lips touch mine. Since we're on a couch he's right next to me and can easily lean into my body. He quickly dips his tongue between my parted lips and pulls back with a smile. "Delicious."

I blush. "That's not what I meant when I asked if you were going to try it."

He wraps his arm behind me and begins tracing circles on the small of my back with his thumb. He leans over my ear and whispers, "Are you complaining about my methods?"

I shiver as he licks my earlobe. "No."

He places feather light kisses along the nape of my neck. "Dev?"

"Hmm?"

"Do you want to go downstairs?"

I bite my lip to stifle a moan. "So bad."

He stands with a smile, pulls some money out of his wallet and places it on the table next to our barely eaten dessert. He leads me back to the elevator without a word as I follow in a haze of lust. He presses the button for the tenth floor as we step into the car. Our bodies vibrate with anticipation as we stare at each other on the short ride down. He gently pushes me forward by the small of my back as we exit to the left.

"Room ten-oh-eight," he says.

We find our room about halfway down the hall and Riley stops to dig in his pocket for the keycard. He swipes it through and the green light illuminates. Turning the knob he says, "You ready?"

I gulp. "Ready as I'll ever be."

RILEY

I OPEN THE DOOR to our room and guide her in by pushing on the small of her back once again. This is definitely my new favorite spot on her body. It dips in perfectly where I rest my hand right above the tempting curve of her ass, making my fingers itch to slide south. Devyn gasps upon seeing my final surprise. Red rose petals are strewn across the white down comforter with a silver bucket of iced champagne and two flutes sitting on the nightstand.

"Oh, Riley," she whispers. My dick stirs at the sound of

her voice. I hope that it's only the first of many times she will say my name tonight with such reverence.

She walks throughout the room, lightly touching her fingertips to each surface. She fits perfectly in such a classy space and I can't help but sit here and admire the view.

"Do you approve?" I ask.

She turns around with that magnificent grin from earlier and replies, "It's perfect."

I walk over to the nightstand and see that the champagne has already been corked so I pour two glasses. Holding one out towards her I say, "Would you like some?"

She smirks. "Why, Mr. McIntyre, are you trying to get me drunk?"

I laugh. "Right! You and I both know who can drink whom under the table here and it certainly isn't me."

She grins as she takes the glass from my hand. "Touché." After a lengthy sip she adds, "What now?"

I step towards her, loving the pink hue that hasn't really left her skin tonight. I gently slide my finger underneath the thick strap of her dress before trailing it down her arm. It's pretty hard to miss the goose bumps that have formed everywhere I've touched. "*Now*, is when you officially have to stop asking questions and just follow my lead."

She gulps. "Oh…um, okay. Can I just have a minute…to you know, freshen up?"

I smile. "Take all the time you need."

NINE

DEVYN

I GRAB MY BAG and head to the bathroom. Once the door is closed, I turn towards the mirror above the marble vanity and take a good look at myself. This is the last time I will see myself as a virgin. Am I really going to do this? I take a deep breath to strengthen my resolve. Yes…yes, I'm definitely going to do this. I questioned my decision to ask Riley a time or two, but any inkling of doubt that was left went out the window after the day we've had. I can't believe how much thought and effort he put into this! I know for a fact that he's never pulled out the stops like this for any other woman, which is probably why I was so caught off guard. Riley doesn't have to woo a woman. Hell, he didn't have to woo me but if I'm being honest with myself, I'm so glad he did.

Mission accomplished, Rye. There is no way I will ever forget this day or regret my decision to make him my first. I can't imagine anyone else making this any better. I pull my dress over my head and hang it on the back of the door. I briefly close my eyes as I step out of my shoes, then reopen them, trying to see myself as Riley will in a matter of minutes. My blonde hair falls past my shoulders in waves, barely touching the slight swell of my breasts. My white lingerie may seem a bit cliché with the whole virginal aspect, but I knew I had to have it the second I saw it. It toes the line between sexy and slutty, but at the same time, it's unequivocally feminine. The barely there lace cups of my bra and matching boy shorts scream anything but purity. I may as well walk out there completely naked for as much as this conceals. Or doesn't conceal, rather. My eyes are drawn to the script embedded on my rib cage. I got my one and only tattoo on my eighteenth birthday and never told a soul about it. I intentionally put it somewhere that could be hidden with clothing. I wonder how he'll react when he reads the words, considering they're so eerily similar to his own.

Time to find out. I take one more deep breath as I twist the door handle.

RILEY

I'M INSTANTLY ON ALERT as I hear the bathroom door opening, then I'm frozen in place the second Devyn comes into view. I drink her in from head to toe and wonder what the hell I did to get so damn lucky. She's fucking perfect. I know I should stop staring like a schmuck and say something but words fail me.

My eyes travel from the pink blush on her cheeks to her pouty lips. They go further down to her tits that are barely encased by a scrap of highly transparent white lace. Her nipples pebble under my gaze making my dick even harder. I wet my lips as I imagine tracing my tongue down her flat stomach and around her belly button. I'm momentarily distracted by something on her left rib. A tattoo? Why didn't I know about that? I smirk as I add her ink to my tongue-tracing agenda and wonder what else she's been hiding from me. I continue my ocular descent until I reach the sexiest motherfucking panties I have ever seen. In my experience, even the lace ones like these have a tighter weave to them, but not Devyn's. Every beautiful part of her body that I'm dying to devour is fully on display. I almost embarrass myself by blowing my load when I get to the center of her body and notice a dark blonde strip of curls. My fists clench and unclench, impatiently waiting to touch every inch of her skin.

She wrings her hands, something she does when she's nervous. "Riley, say something."

I'm shaken out of my stupor. "My God, woman."

She fidgets even more. "Too much?" She crosses her arms over her chest. "I'm sorry; I just wanted something that made me feel sexy. It's stupid and trashy, isn't it?"

I quickly launch into action to squash these ridiculous insecurities of hers. Uncrossing her arms and nodding towards her body I say, "*That* could never be considered stupid or trashy. I'm pretty sure it's the best damn idea you've ever had."

She laughs. "Really?"

I nod enthusiastically. "Uh huh, definitely. Best. Idea. Ever."

She disarms me yet again with her smile. "Well, I'm glad you think so." Resuming her fidgeting she adds, "God, why is this so awkward?"

I shake my head, taking her by both hands. I have to try harder than my dick is at the moment to maintain eye contact so she takes me seriously. "Not awkward, Dev. Just new territory for us." I look down at my fully clothed self. "I appear to be overdressed. Would it help if I evened the playing field?"

She nods. "Yeah, I think so."

I pull my t-shirt over my head and give her a moment to look her fill. I'm not a gym rat by any means but I definitely take care of myself. She reaches out tentatively and runs the tips of her fingers over my pecs. Fuck. Giving her a minute to explore was a bad idea. I swear I can feel my impending orgasm coming at me like a freight train. I still her hand and warn, "Honey, if you keep touching me like that, this will be over before it begins."

She retracts her hand. "What?" After a few seconds it sinks in. "Oh. But...but I thought the more sex you had, the greater your...you know, stamina is."

I laugh. "Typically, my stamina is the last thing you need to worry about, babe. But right now, I feel like a fucking virgin myself when I look at you like this." I hold her jaw in my hand and stroke her cheek with my thumb. "Don't worry, baby. I'll make sure you're well taken care of. And if I happen to...get a little *too* excited the first time, we'll just have to try again... and again...and again until we get it right."

"You can do that?" she says and blushes.

"With you? Yeah, I can definitely do that."

TEN

DEVYN

OH MY GOD. I thought only fictional guys could go for more than one round per night. I know Riley well enough to know that he would never boast about something like that if it weren't possible. Yikes!

"Can I do it more than once tonight? I mean...won't I be too sore or something?"

He smiles. "Maybe...I'm not exactly an expert on de-virginizing someone, Dev. If you are, there's plenty of other things we can do. You're mine for the night and I plan on taking full advantage of that."

I laugh. "Oh yeah?"

He runs his hands down my spine, creating goose pimples everywhere he touches. The look he gives me has me frozen in place. "Yeah." Kissing down my neck he adds, "Now stop thinking. *Feel*."

. . .

RILEY

I START KISSING HER neck while trailing my fingers up and down her back. She walks backwards towards the bed and stops when the back of her knees hit the mattress. I unclasp her bra as I'm gently lowering her down. I slide the white straps down her arms and drop the garment on the floor. Fuck, her tits are amazing. I mold them with my hands, plucking at the pebbled pink tips. I'll admit, before now, I'd say that I definitely preferred a woman with bigger breasts. Devyn's are a little less than a handful but as I take one pert nipple into my mouth, I can't imagine wanting any others.

She arches her back as I begin to suck. "Oh, Riley! God, that feels good."

She writhes beneath me as I pay the other one the same attention and I'm loving every second of it. I tease her more and more with every little whimper. I kiss down her abdomen and stop when I reach her tattoo. I pull back a little to read the words that wrap around her rib cage.

Love deeper and laugh harder than you ever thought possible. Never settle for anything less.

"When did you get this?" I ask as I trace the words with my tongue.

"Eighteenth birthday," she gasps. "You have the most talented tongue!"

I smile against her skin. "You think so?"

She nods her head. "Uh huh. Definitely."

I move lower to show her what I can *really* do with my tongue. She tenses as I reach her panties. "Relax, baby." I kiss along the seam before hooking my fingers under the waistband. "I'm going to taste you now. I need to feel you come apart on my tongue."

"Riley!" she screams as I lower the lace just enough to give her one long lick down the center.

I roll her panties down her legs, toss them aside then drop to my knees. My hands slide under her ass and I open her up to me. I lower my head and lick long and slowly. Her heated flesh is so soft against my tongue and she tastes so fucking sweet I can hardly stand it. There's a light sheen of sweat on her skin, intensifying her sugary scent. Her thighs quiver against my shoulders as I continue licking and sucking her swollen nub. I trace my index finger down her slit and push inside. She grinds her eager body into me, begging for more, so I add another one.

I'm dying to bury myself inside of her as I pump my fingers in and out. It's never been this hard to hold back and never more important that I do so. She clutches the back of my head, pulling me closer while I use my lips and tongue with small nips from my teeth to bring her closer to completion.

"God, I could eat you all day," I murmur against her pink, swollen flesh.

"If you keep doing it like that, I might let you!" she shouts.

My cock is begging to be free of its denim prison. I use my free hand to pop the button and lower the zipper. I can feel that she's close so I pull her legs over my shoulders and tilt her pelvis up for a better angle to continue my ministrations. Her head drops back as she tightens her grip on my hair. I can sense that she's ready so I suck hard and hold on lightly with my teeth. She's screaming my name repeatedly as her thighs clamp down around my skull and her orgasm rips through her. Her body is clenching around my fingers while she pulses against my mouth. I soften my tongue but don't stop licking until the last waves of her climax subside. I rest my head on her stomach for a few seconds to catch my breath. A smile forms as I replay the last ten minutes in my head. *Devyn is a screamer.* Definitely not what I was expecting.

"That was sooo sooo good," she pants. "Like, best orgasm ever!"

I chuckle as I work my way back up her body with kisses. "I'm glad you approve."

She grabs my face and pulls me up so our lips are mere inches apart. "I more than approve, Rye. Seriously, that was incredible." She gets a sly smile on her face. "I think you started out a little strong though...I don't know how you're going to top that."

"Is that a challenge?" I laugh. I don't know what I was expecting but it certainly wasn't this. Any previous awkwardness has gone missing. This girl is giving me shit after I just gave her a screaming orgasm. If it were anyone else, I might be offended. With her, it's fucking hot.

She lifts her head just enough to bite my lower lip. "What if it is?" Fuck, now she's asked for it. That little smartass comment just made my dick even harder.

I slide my hand down and pinch her ass. "You little minx." I brush my hands over her ribs making her squirm.

Her eyes widen when she figures out what I'm thinking. "Don't you dare!"

I wiggle my fingers over her ribs. "What's wrong, Dev? Does that tickle?"

"Ah!" she screams as I step it up. "Don't! No-no-no-no-no!" She's laughing so hard her eyes are watering.

I instantly stop and take her face in my hands. "You are so fucking beautiful, Devyn."

She sobers quickly and meets my eyes. "Rye—"

I silence her with a kiss. Hard and demanding, showing

her how much I need her. I fumble with my jeans until I kick them off. I know she's not ready yet so I leave my boxers on to keep myself in check. She takes everything I give with my mouth, my tongue, and gives it right back to me. Our hands are everywhere, greedily grabbing onto anything we can to gain purchase.

I groan as she wraps her hand around my dick under my boxers. I unconsciously thrust into her fist as she tightens her grip. I'm going to come all over the inside of my shorts if she doesn't stop right now. "Baby, you need to stop that. You feel so fucking good, I'm going to lose my shit. I need to be inside of you when I come."

ELEVEN

DEVYN

WHAT IS HAPPENING TO me? Sure, so far we haven't done anything I haven't done before, but this is different. With Rye, I feel completely out of control. I've never been aggressive with a guy, but with him, all I *am* is want. Need. I should be totally weirded out that Riley and I are naked together but instead, I simply can't get enough of him. I want to touch every inch of his nakedness and I want him to do the same to me.

I stroke his hard length again. "So hurry up and get inside of me."

His eyes widen at my brazen command. "You're not ready yet."

I roll my eyes as he begins circling my clit with the pad of his thumb. "Rye, please. I'm soo, soo ready."

He dips a finger towards my entrance, spreading my wetness around. "Okay, maybe you are. But you need to tell me if it hurts too much…or if I'm coming on too strong. Okay?"

I rise up on my elbows. "I promise."

He pulls back and starts digging through his discarded jeans. Right before I ask him what he's doing, he produces a square foil packet and rips it open with his teeth. He removes his boxers and starts stroking himself. God, that's hot.

I grab his wrist. "Can I put it on?"

He groans. "You're killing me." He takes a deep breath and nods while handing it to me.

I take the condom out of the wrapper and frown. "How do I—is there some sort of trick to this?"

He laughs and guides my hand towards his body. "It's easy. Just pinch the tip and then roll it down as far as it will go."

I close my fingers on the reserve and position the condom over the head of his beautiful erection. I know that's a strange word to use when describing a penis, but his really should be painted on a canvas or something. He jerks as I roll it down his shaft until I reach the base. I slide my hand over his length to ensure that it's on correctly, fascinated by each ridge and vein beneath my palm. He's so thick I can't fully close my hand around him which starts making me a little nervous.

I stroke him once more for good measure. "Did I do it right?"

He groans and tilts his head back. "It's fucking perfect."

I give him a wry smile. "I was talking about the condom, Riley."

He looks down and briefly inspects my work. "That's good too."

I bite my lip. "So, we're good to go?"

His dimples are in full effect. "We are *so* good to go."

Riley hooks his arms behind me and moves us towards

the center of the bed. He starts kissing my neck again moving downward.

"Rye, what are you doing?"

He grabs a rose petal. "Shh, stop thinking so much."

He drags the velvety soft petal over my collarbone from left to right, slowly making his way over to my breast. I gasp when he circles my nipple then closes his mouth over the peak. He moves the petal lower while his mouth never leaves my breast. I'm so lost in the moment that I startle when he brushes his thumb over my sensitive bud.

He lifts his head, fusing our mouths together while his thumb continues to circle that same spot over and over. I writhe beneath him as he works my body into a frenzy. Everything he's doing is so wonderful but I need...more. I'm aching to be filled by him.

"Riley, please!"

"Shh, baby. I'll take care of you." I feel him lining up against my entrance. He looks up to meet my eyes and says, "Are you ready?"

I nod. "Please, Rye. I need more."

He smiles and takes my face into his hands. I'm so slick that he pushes in slightly with little effort but halts when I stiffen from the pressure. "You okay?"

I look him in the eyes and nod. "Yeah, I'm just nervous."

He kisses the corners of my mouth and moves his hand lower. He traces circles over my nub as he whispers soothing words to help me relax. "It's okay, baby. I've got you. This is perfectly natural. It's just you and me here. Do you trust me?"

I moan as he continues rubbing. "You know I do."

"I'm going to push in all the way now. Okay?"

I can see the veins protruding on his forehead from the control he's exerting. "Okay."

He tucks his head into the crook of my neck as he slowly

inches himself forward. It burns but it's not unbearable. I've used a vibrator before but it didn't fill me nearly as much as Riley does. There's a pinch right as he seats himself to the hilt which makes me wince a little.

He pauses. "You okay?"

I take a deep breath. "Uh huh."

He lifts his head and looks down to where our bodies are joined. He guides my hand lower until I can feel the spot where we connect. "Do you feel that? We're in this together. Do you feel how wet you are? Your body wants this, baby. You need to stop thinking so hard and just *feel*." He pulls back slightly and pushes forward again. "Look how easy that was. It's like your body was fucking made for me. God, you feel so fucking good, Devyn."

He moves in and out a little further. The pressure isn't so bad this time. Riley palms my breast and begins kneading it as he trails kisses down my neck. I arch my back when he pinches my nipple. It's like there's a direct line to what's happening down below. The burning sensation lets up as he continues to thrust slowly. I feel incredibly full, but the combination of what he's doing above and below the waist-line is a heady thing. My hand is still trapped between our bodies so each time he slides in and out, he brushes the tips of my fingers. The eroticism of it pushes me over the precipice of discomfort straight into pleasure.

He lifts his head. "How you doing, baby? Are you okay?"

I wrap my legs around his hips, pulling him closer. "I'm *so* good, Rye."

RILEY

. . .

I SWEAR TO GOD, her body feels like it was molded just for mine. No pussy has ever felt as good as Devyn's does. She's so tight and so fucking responsive. Her body sings with every kiss, touch, and stroke that I deliver. After the first few thrusts, she became slicker than a gallon of lube. My dick slides in and out of her with ease as I work her body over with everything that I've got.

"Riley," she pants, "go faster. *Please* go faster."

Mother fuck. If I go any faster, I'm going to turn into a two-pump chump. "No, baby. We need to take this one nice and slow."

She claws my back and digs her heels into my ass. "Riley! Please! I need it harder!"

Yep, that did it! Who am I to deny this woman? I angle myself a little better, pulling her legs a little higher on my hips. Then I hunker down and give the lady what she wants. I progressively move faster and harder until we're both dripping with sweat and gasping for air. Devyn meets me thrust for thrust, clawing my back, screaming for more the entire time. This woman is a wildcat. I would've never, *ever* expected such a reaction from her. It's the hottest fucking experience of my existence.

When I feel myself about to blow, I move my hand lower. I'm determined to make her come at least once more before I do. I coat my fingers in her juices and circle that little bundle of nerves repeatedly, bringing her to the edge.

"Riley, I'm going to come!" she screams.

Her pussy pulses as she screams through her orgasm. "Oh fuck, Devyn!" I follow right behind her as her body clenches me tighter than I ever thought possible.

"Oof!" she says as I collapse on top of her with dead weight.

I grab the condom and pull out slowly, rolling to the side. "Sorry, you just milked every ounce of energy I had."

She laughs and continues breathing heavily. "Ditto."

I grab a tissue from the nightstand, wrap the condom inside, and toss it in the trash closest to the bed. I face her and take a moment to soak her in. She's lying on her back with her eyes closed, an arm hooked over her head. Her skin is flushed and slick with sweat, her hair is a mess, and her eye makeup is smudged but she's never been hotter. She must sense me staring because she opens her eyes and smiles directly at me. I half expected her to cover herself but she continues to lie in the same position with no inhibitions whatsoever. This woman never ceases to amaze me.

"Are you okay?" I ask.

She rolls towards me and tucks her hands under her chin. "Rye, that was…God, there are no words. Thank you."

I tuck a loose hair behind her ear and smile. "No, *thank you*. For trusting me. For giving me something so special. Sex has never been like that for me."

She crinkles her brow. "What do you mean?"

I think for a minute. "It's like you said…there are no words. But if I had to try, I'd say that I've never felt so in tune with someone before. Maybe it's because we know each other so well…I don't know. All I do know is that it was fucking amazing."

Her eyes light up. "Really?"

"Really," I assure her. I climb out of bed and extend my hand. "Come with me."

She looks confused. "Um…I'm not really dressed to go anywhere."

I laugh as I pull her off the mattress and lead her into the bathroom. She watches silently while I run the water in the large soaker tub. I look over my shoulder and say, "The warm water should help with any soreness."

She grins. "You really did think of everything, didn't you?"

I guide her into the tub and settle in behind her. Pulling her back into my chest I say, "The Boy Scouts taught me to be prepared for anything."

She chuckles. "Well kudos to them for that."

We soak in the tub for a while, perfectly content not saying a word. I start rubbing her shoulders and finally break the silence. "So, did the second orgasm top the first?"

"Hmm...I don't know. I think it was too close to call. Maybe I need another one to decide."

I laugh. "Oh yeah?" My hands move lower, caressing her. "Do you think you're up for that?"

She gasps. "Well, maybe not the actual sex. At least not for a bit. But I'm open to other stuff..."

I smile against her hair and start rubbing her shoulders again. "Anything specific on your mind?"

She moans and wiggles her ass against my dick. "Mmm, keep doing that and I'll do anything you want."

I'm instantly rock hard and ready to go. "Fuck, Dev. You're not making this easy on me. I'm trying to be a gentleman here. When you say shit like that, gentle is the last thing on my mind."

She turns around and straddles my lap in all her wet naked glory. "Maybe I don't want to be handled like glass. I'm tougher than I look, you know."

Our eyes meet. She's hiding something in those hypnotizing hazel eyes. I recall the words permanently etched into her skin. "What's with the tattoo?"

Her eyes widen. "Oh, it's just something someone said to me once. It stuck with me."

I narrow my eyes at her. "I'm going to go ahead and call bullshit on that."

Her eyes follow my hand as I trace the letters with my index finger. "What? Why?"

"Because you don't do *anything* without a purpose. These words? They mean something to you. Something big."

She sighs. "My mom said them. Before she died, she wrote letters to me for every big occasion in my life. The day I got my first period, the day I went on my first date, the day I become a mom...stuff like that. She wanted to be there for me...in spirit anyway. I think she knew deep down my dad would never remarry. She wanted me to have a female perspective for the important stuff."

I tuck a wet strand behind her ear. "Which occasion were these words from?"

"Eighteenth birthday. I read the letter and went straight to a tattoo shop. It's the only truly impulsive thing I've done in my entire life."

I run my hands over her rib cage. "You should try being impulsive more often. You never know what could happen."

She smiles and unplugs the drain. Stepping out of the tub she says, "Why don't we go work on that together?"

TWELVE

DEVYN

RILEY AND I ARE lying in bed, completely spent. He's the big spoon and I'm the little. We had sex two more times and each one was better than the last. I never thought losing my virginity would be such a pleasurable experience. I knew Riley would make it as good as possible but I never expected to feel so delightfully sated. Sure, I'm sore; I probably will be for days. But it's a delicious soreness.

I think back to everything that's happened tonight and smile. It was so perfect. Riley is not only skilled but also a generous lover. No wonder he's had so many girlfriends. I cringe when I think about the bevy of babes from his past. I've never really liked any of the women he's dated, but I put up with them knowing that they had a short shelf life. Now look at me. I'm another notch on the bedpost just like them.

I mentally shake my head, refusing to put myself in the same category. I know what Riley and I shared tonight was special. Different. He even said that he's never been so in sync with someone before. Riley and I are so attuned to each other outside of the bedroom that it makes sense it would carry over. He tightens his arms around me and I nuzzle into him. God, I could get used to this. I know I said I didn't have time for a relationship but loving Riley is so effortless. And the fact that we're so compatible sexually is just the icing on the cake. Wait…did I just say I love Riley? Well, of course I love him. But am I *in love* with him? Oh crap, I am! I totally am! If I'm being honest with myself, I have been for years. I've just always had this wall in place preventing me from going there in my head. But tonight, any barriers we had were broken down and then some.

Why couldn't I have had this epiphany sooner? Would he even want a relationship with me now? Could we have one being three thousand miles away? My internship only lasts for one year. Maybe I could move to Boston until Riley finishes grad school then we could figure it out from there. We'll both be so busy, time will probably fly by. I decide to take Riley's advice and act on impulse.

"Hey, Rye?" I whisper.

"Hmm?" he mumbles sleepily.

"I love you."

He doesn't say anything so I shift to see his face. His eyes are closed and his breathing is even. Is he asleep? A soft snore confirms it. What's the proper protocol here? Should I wake him up? He looks so peaceful…I don't want to disturb him. I roll back over and close my eyes. We can talk after we've both had some rest.

RILEY

"I LOVE YOU."

. . .

Fuck. Why did she have to say that? I focus on taking deep, even breaths so she thinks I'm asleep. I even add a little snore when I feel her turn towards me. Yep, I'm a total asshole. But what the fuck am I supposed to do? Sex wasn't supposed to change things between us. We had a deal! I've just had the best night of my entire life and she had to ruin it by dropping the L word. What's she thinking? I'm freaking the fuck out right now. Okay, so maybe I have...*feelings* for her too. She's my best friend. Of course I feel affection for her. But love? That's insane. I can't be in love with someone when I'm moving across the country. I'm not a relationship type of guy. Especially not a long distance relationship. There's no way I could ever be the man she deserved. I don't do monogamy. Not for more than a few weeks at a time anyway. She knows this. What the fuck was she thinking telling me she loves me? I am clawing at my insides for an answer. What am I supposed to do? The only thing I can think of is pretend I didn't hear her. That's the most diplomatic way of handling this, right? I'll remind her in the morning what this weekend was all about before she has a chance to broach the subject again. Then we'll go back to being friends and everything's good. Easy, right?

THIRTEEN

DEVYN

SUNLIGHT SLICES THROUGH THE room, effectively ending my deep sleep. The absence of heat from Riley's body clues me in to the fact that he's missing before I even turn over to confirm it. I listen for any signs of him in the bathroom. I sit up when I realize that I'm the only one in our room. Where the heck is he? He wouldn't have just left in the middle of the night, right? No, that's ridiculous.

I look around as my eyes adjust to the brightness and find a note on the nightstand.

Good morning, beautiful. Went to get coffee. Be back soon.
-RM

I smile at his thoughtfulness. Riley knows I can't function before having at least one cup of coffee. I decide to take a quick shower to freshen up before he returns. As I exit the bathroom wearing nothing but the hotel-issued robe, I find him leaning against the dresser.

I smile. "Hey."

"Hey." He holds up two cups from Starbucks. "I thought you might need some caffeine before heading back to your apartment."

I grab one and take a healthy sip. "Mmm, you thought right."

I think he groaned. "Uh…good."

I cock my head to the side and study him. He looks uncomfortable. "You okay?"

He chokes a little on the sip he was taking. "What? Uh, yeah. Why wouldn't I be?"

Okay, why is he being so twitchy? Is this normal morning after behavior? Does he regret last night? "You're acting weird, Riley. What's going on?"

He clears his throat. "Weird? Huh. I don't feel weird. I think you're letting your imagination get the best of you, Dev."

I put my hand on my hip. "Spill it, Rye. Why are you being so cagey? Do you regret what happened last night?"

He looks shocked. "What? God, no." He sets his coffee on the dresser and walks over to me. "Why would you ask that? *Do you have regrets?*"

I shake my head and make direct eye contact. "Not a single one."

He smiles. "Well, then we're in agreement. No regrets."

RILEY

. . .

OKAY, THIS IS IT. I need to cut off any chance of the L word showing its face again. I grab her coffee out of her hand and place it next to mine. I don't feel like being scalded if this goes downhill. "Last night was fun. A lot of fun."

"Fun?" she repeats.

I employ the panty-melting grin. "Sure. I had a great time. Didn't you?"

She scowls. "You could say that…"

I can see her mind working overtime. She's always been an open book around me. She's wondering if I heard her last night. She's wondering if she should bring it up. That would be a hell no. Time to finish this.

I grab my bag, sling it over my shoulder, and place her car keys in her palm. "Here's your keys. I need to get back to school. There's been a change of plans. My parents called while I was getting coffee. They're coming into town a bit early to help me box up all my stuff before graduation."

Her jaw drops. "You're leaving? How are you getting home?"

I shrug. "I'm taking the train. They're going to pick me up from the station in Eugene."

"Oh," she says in barely more than a whisper. "So, I guess I'll see you when I get back tomorrow then?"

"Maybe…I'll be pretty busy with my folks. They want to load all my stuff into our trucks before grad so we can leave right after the ceremony. I'm going back to Napa with them for a short visit before heading out to Boston."

She looks dumbfounded. "And this was all planned during your coffee run?"

The story was. My parents really are on their way but they won't be in town until tomorrow morning. "Huh? No,

I've been planning to spend a few days in Napa for weeks now. I'm sure I must've told you."

She gulps. "It must've slipped your mind."

I shrug. "My bad."

She sits on the end of the bed. "So...I guess I'll see you when I see you?"

I place my hand on the doorknob. "Yep. I'll see ya later. Thanks for a fun night, Dev."

I think she muttered something as I closed the door but I'm not positive.

FOURTEEN

6 WEEKS LATER

DEVYN

I'M JUST ABOUT TO step out for lunch when I feel a sudden wave of nausea. I spot the ladies' room up ahead and increase my pace. As soon as I make it to the stall, I lose the contents of my stomach and heave until there's nothing left. I hear the restroom door open as I'm hunched over and try to remain as quiet as possible.

There's a small knock on the stall. "Hey, Devyn. It's Andrea. Are you okay? I saw you run in here and I heard... well, it sounds like you're throwing up."

Andrea is from Human Resources. She welcomed me to the agency on the first day of my internship and helped me fill out all the appropriate new hire paperwork.

I wipe my mouth with some toilet paper. "I think so. I'll be out in just a sec."

I step out of the stall after flushing. I wash my hands and dig into my purse for my little travel bottle of mouthwash. As I'm swishing the contents around in my mouth I think about how thankful I am for being so prepared. Some people give me crap about my incessant need to plan for everything but it works for me.

"Are you sure you're okay?" Andrea asks as she's freshening up her lipstick.

I spit into the sink. "Yeah, I'm sorry; I don't know where that came from. I felt fine and then all of a sudden, my breakfast was in the toilet. I feel better now."

She looks at me through the mirror. "You're not pregnant, are you? When my sister was pregnant with her first, she would get sick one minute and be ready to scarf down an entire buffet the next. It was nuts."

"What?" I sputter. "Uh, no, definitely not pregnant." Okay, so my period is late but that's not uncommon for me. Especially not when I'm super stressed from all the long hours I've been working over the past few weeks.

Andrea looks skeptical. "Are you sure? People don't normally puke without reason. Have you taken a test?"

I start reapplying my lip gloss. "I'm sure. I haven't had sex in a while...and when I did, we used a condom. Several of them."

Andrea smiles. "So did my sister, Julia. With her first *and* third kid. Condoms break. I'm just saying it wouldn't hurt to stop by the drug store on your way home."

I try to push back the panic. Could she be right? "Thanks, Andrea. I'll consider that."

RILEY

"DUDE, WILL YOU QUIT looking like someone just ran over your dog?" Brody whines. "You're a shitty wingman." Brody started his master's program during the summer semester like I did. We share a lot of the same classes and recently started hanging out.

I take a swig of beer. "Sorry, man. I'm just distracted."

"About what?"

I take another drink. "It's nothing."

"Uh oh," he says. "I know that look. Tell me about her."

I look up. "What?"

He laughs. "The chick. You're hung up on a chick. So tell me about her. Is she hot? How big are her tits?"

I sigh. "Is it that obvious?"

He claps me on the back. "Totally obvious. Who is she? Have I seen her around campus?"

I shake my head. "No. She's from back home. Well, from U of O, where I did my undergrad. We were really good friends for years but never hooked up until right before I left town. I haven't talked to her since and I feel like a dick."

"Why not? Did she get all clingy or something?"

I think back to that night. Yeah, she dropped the L word, but she was just being honest, not clingy. "No, man. She didn't. It was just best to make a clean break."

"Why? Was the sex awful?"

"Best sex of my life."

He smiles. "Ah, I get it, brother. You've been touched by the Magic Pussy."

"The magic *what?*"

"The Magic Pussy," he repeats. "Pussy that is so good you can never get enough and it's impossible to forget. An Urban Legend in my opinion, but you sure do have all the pathetic signs."

"Thanks," I grumble. Sounds about right though.

"Seriously, though. Are we talking apples, oranges, or is she packing a pair of melons?"

I roll my eyes. "Quit talking about her tits, man."

His jaw drops. "Oh man, you're worse off than I

thought. You don't even want another guy talking about her tits. I can't imagine what you'd do to the poor sap that *touches* them."

I think about another man touching Devyn's *anything* and glare. "Shut the fuck up, man."

He holds his hands up in defense. "Hey, buddy. I'm just speaking the truth here. If you're still thinking about her almost two months after the fact, why don't you just call her?"

"It's not that simple."

Brody shrugs. "Your call, dude, but quit killing my prospects here. At least try to look like you want to be here."

FIFTEEN

DEVYN

"NO-NO-NO-NO-NO-NO-NO-NO-NO." I'M SITTING ON my bathroom floor surrounded by seven pregnancy tests. Seven! All positive. I couldn't believe it when the first one showed a little pink plus sign. I thought for sure it was defective so I went back to the drugstore and bought six more— one from each different brand they had in stock. What am I going to do? How could this have happened? This isn't part of the plan! Sure, I want kids some day but not before I have the chance to establish a career, or get married. What am I going to do?

I take a few deep breaths while staring at the digital sign that reads, *Pregnant*. I grab my phone off the counter and scroll to Riley's name. We haven't spoken since the hotel. I'd called him quite a few times before graduation but they all went to voicemail. I also tried Josh, but he blew me off too, saying that Rye was just really busy. I tried finding him at graduation but there were too many people. I watched him accept his diploma and walk off stage. That's the last time I saw him. How am I supposed to tell him that I'm pregnant? We're on opposite sides of the country! He still has two years of school left. And what about my internship? Crap! Crap! Crap! Wouldn't one of us have noticed if the condom broke?

I bite the bullet and hit the call button. It rings four times before it's answered.

"Hello, Riley's phone!" a girl slurs.

I hold the phone away from my ear. Is this really happening right now? Who is this chick answering his phone? Why is there so much background noise?

"Hello, is Riley available?"

"No, he's not. That big ball of hot man is getting me another drink. Can I take a message?"

"No, no message." I hang up quickly, feeling sick, and wind up puking *again*. As I lay on the cold tile floor, I sob. What am I going to do? Riley's obviously back to his old manwhore ways. Our night together clearly didn't have the same significance to him as it did to me. How can we raise a baby together when he won't even talk to me?

RILEY

I SCOWL WHEN I see the annoying brunette setting my phone down on the table. "What are you doing with my phone?"

"It rang," she slurs. "I answered it."

I pick up my phone and scroll through the caller ID. *Devyn.* "What did she say? What did you say to her?" I growl.

"I said hello, some chick asked for you, I said you were getting me a drink and offered to take a message. She didn't want to leave one."

"What *exactly* did she say?" I yell.

"Whoa, dude, calm down," Brody says as he joins us at the table.

I fling my arm out. "This bimbo thought she should answer my phone! I was trying to find out what the caller said."

"Hey!" she whined. "Who are you calling a bimbo?"

Her friend shot me a look of disgust. "Who do you think you are, asshole?" She looked at Brody and pouted. "Brody bear, are you going to let him talk to my friend like that?"

Brody bear? Oh geez.

"Uh…" he stammers.

She stands up and huffs. "You know what? You're an asshole just like your friend! Find someone else to suck you off tonight!"

Both women stomp away.

Brody punches me in the arm. "Way to cock block, bro. Rachel has mad head-giving skills. I think my dick actually whimpered as she was walking away. What gives?"

I sigh. "I'm sorry, man. That girl I was telling you about earlier called while I was at the bar. Drunkie McGee decided to answer my phone and said God knows what to her. She probably thinks we're fucking or something."

"Who cares what she's thinking?" Brody says. "You said a clean break was for the best, right? If that's true, then it's a good thing if she thinks you've already moved on. Right?"

I take a sip of my beer and swallow the bitterness. I don't know if it's the ale or regret that's causing the lump in my throat. "Right."

Part
TWO

5 Years Later

SIXTEEN

RILEY

BRODY POINTS TO ME as I walk into the sports bar he asked me to meet him at. "There he is!"

I join him at the pool table and nod to the guy he's playing against.

"Riley, this is Drew." Brody nods to me. "And Drew, this is my buddy from grad school, Riley. He just moved to Seattle."

I shake hands with Drew. "Nice to meet you, man."

"You too." Drew picks up his pool cue. "Eight ball side pocket." He sinks the ball. "Ha! Take that bitch!"

"Damn it!" Brody says.

I laugh at Brody's pouty expression. "Tough luck, asshole."

Brody responds with a two-finger salute.

"Not tonight baby. I have a headache," I retort.

Drew laughs, takes Brody's pool stick, and hands it to me.

"You want a beer? Brody is buying the next round because his sorry ass can't sink any balls."

I smirk at Brody. "You'd think he'd be a ball expert since he plays with his own all day long."

"Fuck you, dick," Brody laughs.

"Ha!" Drew says. "I like you, Riley! You want to play? I could use an actual opponent."

"What the fuck? Is this pick on Brody day?" Brody asks.

Drew looks around the bar. "I don't see any other whiny bitches around here."

"Fuck both of you dickheads," Brody mutters as he walks over to the bar.

I laugh. "So how long have you known Brody?"

Drew racks the balls on the felt. "We were in the same frat. I was his big brother." He nods to the table. "You mind if I break?"

I shake my head. "Go for it."

Brody returns with a pitcher of beer and three glasses. He pours one for himself and takes a seat at a nearby table. "Drew, when's your fine ass sister getting here?"

Drew makes his shot and scowls. "Shut the fuck up, dude."

Brody laughs. "Why? I'm only speaking the truth." He looks at me. "Rye, wait until you meet Drew's little sister. She and her friend always joins us for Monday Night Football. Fuck, I'd give my left nut to be the meat in that sandwich."

"Keep it up, asshole," Drew mutters.

I laugh. "Hot sister, huh?"

Drew points his cue at me. "Don't even think about it. My sister is off limits."

I raise my hands in defense. "It's all good, dude. You don't need to worry about me."

Drew narrows his eyes. "Why not? Are you batting for Team Sausage?"

My eyes widen. "What? No!"

Brody laughs. "Nah, man. Riley's just hung up on the Magic Pussy. Has been for years. This asshole finally nutted up and decided to try winning her back by moving to Seattle."

Drew pats me on the back. "Ah, the elusive Magic Pussy. So this chick lives in Seattle?"

I take a sip of beer. "No, Portland. Seattle is the closest place I could find a job in my field."

Drew nods to Brody. "So you're into airplanes and shit too?"

I laugh. "Yeah, you could say that."

"That's cool," Drew says. "So what's the story with this lady friend of yours?"

"Aw, man, this is good," Brody interrupts. "So, apparently, they were good friends in college, but Riley here decided to try the whole friends with benefits thing their last year in school. Things got weird and they lost contact. I watched him date one hot blonde after another in Boston trying to get over her, but the Magic Pussy always prevailed. Apparently, she smells like baked goods or some shit like that. Riley can't walk into a donut shop without getting a hard-on."

"Shut up, asshat. That's not true," I argue.

Brody laughs. "Right. Why is it that you're not allowed in that Krispy Kreme again?"

I glare at him while Drew hunches over in laughter. "Fuck you, dude."

"Speaking of hot blondes," Brody says. "Seriously, Drew, what time is your sister supposed to show?"

Drew glares at him. "Why do you care?"

Brody shrugs. "Just curious."

I stare at Brody for a few seconds trying to figure him out. "Are you interested in her or something?"

"He'd better not be," Drew says. "He knows the rules. She's off limits."

"Why's that?" I ask.

"She's had a hard time," Drew says. "She's a single mom. Got knocked up the summer after college and the father took off when she told him she was pregnant. She didn't have anyone else so she moved in with me. She's doesn't need any assholes in her life complicating things."

"How long ago was this?" I ask.

"Almost five years now," Drew answers. "She had to give up a kick ass job to move up here when she was pregnant so she didn't have anything at the time. She could've afforded to move out a few years back when she landed another job but I asked her to stay. My nephew needs a man in his life and I've been there since day one. I'm going to really miss the little man when she finally decides to get a place of her own. He's the coolest four-year-old I know."

"Doesn't this dick pay child support?" I ask.

Drew says, "Nope. Real winner, right? The asshole has never even met his kid. Truth is…I think he broke her heart pretty badly so she never tried to pursue any legal action. Out of sight, out of mind, I guess. I've tried talking her into it but she refuses to discuss it. She won't even tell me his name which is probably a good thing since I'd probably end up in jail for murder."

Wow, asshole is right. Brody suddenly whistles loudly because a hot little redhead just walked in.

I raise an eyebrow. "The sister? I thought you said she was blonde."

Brody's eyes haven't left the redhead. "No, sister's friend. That's Rainey. She's fine as fuck but her pussy's locked up tighter than Fort Knox. Believe me…I've tried. Repeatedly."

Drew laughs. "That's because you don't have the right skills."

The woman joins us at the pool table. "Hey guys." She gives me a good once over, the appreciation obvious. "Who's this?"

I extend my hand. "I'm Riley."

She takes my hand. "Hi, handsome. I'm Rainey. How do you know the boys here?"

I nod to Brody. "Brody and I went to grad school together. I'm new to the area and he invited me here to meet some friends."

She smiles. "Really? Well, I'd be happy to show you around sometime."

"Rainey," Brody growls. "Where's—"

"There she is!" Drew interrupts. He waves his hands, signaling someone. "Over here!"

I look up in same direction and choke on my beer when I see the woman he's referring to.

Drew smacks me on the back. "You okay there, bud?"

I slam my closed fist into my chest. "Hey, Drew? What's your last name?"

"Summers. Why?"

Well, what are the odds? I know the moment she recognizes me because she stops dead in her tracks and forms an O with her pouty lips. The same lips that I've pictured wrapped around my dick every day since I last saw her. I set my beer on the table and step forward with a big grin.

"Hi, Dev. Long time no see."

DEVYN

"HI, DEV. LONG TIME no see," Riley says while flashing his perfect dimples, making me a little weak in the knees.

Those dimples are my Kryptonite on the man *and* the

115

boy. The boy he has no idea exists. Correction, the *son* he has no idea exists. Out of every possible situation in which I'd imagined running into him again, this definitely wasn't it. What on Earth is he doing in Seattle? Better yet, why is he hanging out with my brother? Okay, Devyn, woman up and play it cool; you can't just stand here gaping at the man no matter how devastatingly beautiful he still is.

"Riley," I reply as nonchalantly as possible. "Nice to see you again."

Drew looks between the two of us, confusion etched in his features. "You two know each other?"

"Yeah," I reply. "Riley and I knew each other in college." I turn my face away from the man in question so he can't see the blush staining my cheeks.

Drew makes a face. "Ugh! Please do not tell me 'knew each other' is code for 'We got it on like Donkey Kong.'?" He looks sternly at Rye. "Dude, no offense, but I'm going to have to kick your ass if you've seen my baby sister naked."

"Um…" Riley stammers. "We…uh…" He looks to me for help. I could always read his thoughts in college; it was like we shared the same brain sometimes. Apparently, that hasn't changed because he's asking me with his eyes how I want this to play out. Now isn't that a loaded question?

"No, you idiot," I interrupt. "Riley and I were just friends. Acquaintances, really. No nudity involved. I haven't even spoken to him since senior year. By the way, who uses phrases like 'Get it on like Donkey Kong'? I swear Nathan is more mature than you sometimes."

"Phew!" Drew swings a heavy arm around my shoulders, completely ignoring my dig about his maturity level. He then does the same with Riley, hugging us into him, forcing our bodies a little too close for comfort. "Thank fuck! I didn't want there to be any awkwardness. C'mon, lets grab our seats and watch the Seahawks kick ass!"

Right, no awkwardness at all.

SEVENTEEN

RILEY

FRIENDS? NO WAIT, *ACQUAINTENCES?* Damn, so much for hoping she'd let this whole thing blow over. I was counting on the old adage, *time heals all wounds*. Okay, I can understand her not wanting to reveal the fact that she lost her virginity to me, but I think I'm a little insulted that she's not even laying claim to how close we were back then. Fuck thinking I'm insulted; I *am* insulted. She was my best friend and I *know* she felt the same way about me. She was the only woman in my life besides my mom that I ever cared about. Hell, I moved across the country just for the chance of seeing her again. And now she's practically fallen into my lap my first week in town. This has to be more than a crazy coincidence.

Wait a second…is she the sister Drew was talking about? I never met him before today, but I know Devyn only has one sibling. Does she really have a *kid?* He said it's been five years since that asshole had dumped her after she told him she was pregnant. Doing the math in my head, it had to have been shortly after we had slept together. If this dickbag broke her heart, that means that she jumped into a relationship with him *right after* hooking up with me. I guess her 'I love you' was all for show. She really was just interested in popping her cherry then moving on, wasn't she?

Trying to conceal how angry I am, I ask, "So, Devyn... what have you been up to? How long has it been, anyway?"

"I've been great," she replies with a saccharine tone that doesn't match the ball-shriveling glare she is shooting my way. "I don't know...how long *has* it been? Our senior year was about five years ago, I suppose. Isn't it amazing how fast time flies when you're having fun? If I remember correctly, you like to go out and have *a lot of fun*, don't you?"

Ouch. Yeah, so I've slept with a lot of women but I'm nowhere near as bad as I was in college. Sex with random women lost its appeal years ago. It took me six months after being with Devyn before I could even get hard for someone else. And believe me, when you're a twenty-two-year-old guy who could get his dick waxed anywhere, anytime, that's like a fucking lifetime of celibacy. No matter how hot the girl is, it's just not as good as I remember it being before her. That's how my sex life is categorized now: B.D. and A.D. *Before Devyn* and *After Devyn*. I hate admitting that Brody's right, but magic pussy indeed. I remember being so cocky thinking that I'd ruin her for every other man when in reality... *she's* the one who has ruined *me*. I'm such a dumbass.

I'm also a dick, apparently, because I can't help but go for the jugular with my next line of questioning. "So, Drew tells me you have a kid. I guess congratulations are in order. Who's the dad?"

"DUDE!" Drew shouts.

Devyn's face turns beet red as her mouth falls open. She

levels Drew with a look that I can't make sense of and says, "You told him? What the hell, Drew?"

Drew gives me an accusing glare. "Me? If anyone deserves a 'what the hell' it's this asshole! Dude, *what the hell?*"

I hold my hands up in surrender. "I'm sorry. I didn't mean for it to come out that way. I was just curious, I suppose." I stare Devyn directly in the eyes before adding, "You and I were...*hanging out* right before graduation and there was no boyfriend then. I was just wondering when exactly you met this kid's father. Drew said he's four now which would mean you had to start dating him *right after we hung out.* Am I doing the math wrong here?"

"Nope, your genius brain is working just fine." She stands up from the table at which we've just sat. She looks at Drew before adding, "Look, Drew, I'm sorry but I just remembered that Rose has to bail early tonight. I have to get back to Nate and can't stay for the game. I'll see you at home." She stumbles a bit as she starts walking away so I jump up to steady her by the elbow. Is that a tear in her eye? She jerks her arm away. "Bye, Riley."

Her friend gets up to chase after her but not before jabbing me in the chest with her finger. "You should consider wearing a cup next time I see you. That was *not* cool."

I plop back into the booth. "Not cool at all, dude," Drew says.

"I know, man," I agree. "I'm sorry. I'll make it up to her, okay?"

Drew looks skeptical. "You can try, but it's a pretty touchy subject. Just tread lightly, okay? I like you; I don't want to have to kick your ass."

I smile briefly at his warning. "Got it."

DEVYN

. . .

"DEVYN, WAIT UP!" RAINEY shouts as she chases after me. I wipe away the lone tear that escaped before she can reach me.

I stop on the sidewalk and wait for her to catch up. "Lorraine, you didn't have to come after me. I'm fine. You should go back and enjoy the game."

She puts her hand on her hip and gawks at me. "You're *fine*? The fuck you are! What the hell happened back there?"

I sniffle a little. Stupid, girly hormones. "Nothing happened. I just got a little emotional when Riley brought up *he who must not be named*."

"Bullshit! You're on the verge of crying, for fuck's sake!" She throws her hands up in exasperation. "And for the record, 'he who must not be named' is only called that because you refuse to *name* him!"

I sniffle again, making her face soften. "Oh, honey, please don't cry. I don't know what the fuck to do with tears. I grew up with five brothers; there was no crying allowed on Testosterone Island."

I suck back the emotions and paste a smile on my face. "I'm sorry. I feel better now. I must be getting my period or something."

"Periods suck!" she exclaims. "Women totally got screwed in the gender pool. We have to deal with bleeding once a month, we can't pee standing up, and we're expected to blow our vaginas to Smithereens bringing life into the world!" She winces, probably just now remembering who she's talking to. "Oh, I didn't really mean that last one. I'm sure your vagina is beautiful...and tight...not blown out in the least. Guys probably love getting all up in your coochie!"

I roll my eyes. "Okay, can we *please* stop talking about my vagina now?"

"Sure, no more talk about perfectly tight vaginas. Now that reality TV woman that's had like twenty kids is a different story. Her vagina has to be obliterated by this point. Seriously, having sex with her must feel like shooting an arrow down a hallway."

I make a gagging gesture from the visual she's just planted in my brain. "Let me clarify, Lorraine. Can we please stop talking about ALL vaginas now?"

She puts her arm around my shoulders. "C'mon. Let's go get you some chocolate and get you back to that handsome little boy waiting at home."

I smile as we start walking. "That sounds perfect."

EIGHTEEN

RILEY

THANK FUCK IT'S FINALLY Friday. This week has been insane. I've been trying to get settled in my new job during the day while unpacking my shit at night. It's been four days since I've seen Devyn and I'm climbing the walls. The kid thing really threw me off but now that I've had a few days to sit on it, I've decided it doesn't have to change my plans. I came here with the number one goal of getting her back into my life. Yeah, she has a kid, but it's not like I haven't dated anyone these past five years. It could've just as easily happened to me. If she's willing to let me back into her life, I can figure out how to add her offspring into the equation.

It's nine o'clock and I'm starving. My new condo is in the South Lake Union district so thankfully, I have tons of options within walking distance. I have a mad craving for some pasta so I decide to check out the Italian place on the corner.

The hostess greets me with a smile as I walk in the door. "Welcome to Bugatti's. Table for one?"

I shake my head. "No, I'd like to get some takeout."

She grabs a menu and nods. "Follow me. You can order in the bar when you're ready and have a drink while you wait."

I take a seat directly in front of the bartender. "This is Mike," the hostess says. "Let him know when you're ready to order."

I open my menu. "Thanks."

Mike approaches me after a few minutes. "Have you decided?"

I nod. "Yes. I'll have the Lasagna Bolognese to go and a pint of IPA while I wait."

He nods and takes my menu. He pours my beer and sets the chilled glass on the bar. "Very good choice. The lasagna will take about twenty minutes."

DEVYN

I'M TRYING TO FINISH my third glass of Chardonnay when Jackson takes the glass away from me. "Hey, slow down there, Devyn. Since when are you a binge drinker?"

I scowl at him. "It's been a rough week. Can I have my glass back please?"

He hands it back to me. "Fine. But I'm coming home with you afterwards. I'm not comfortable with you being drunk around Nathan."

I roll my eyes. "And you think I would be? Nathan is spending the night at Rainey's. She was complaining about how little time she's had with him lately. She's taking him to the zoo in the morning."

In reality, she knew what a crappy week I've had and wanted to help out. Even though I haven't told her about my past with Riley, she senses something big is going on. Hence, my need for something stronger than wine. Maybe Jackson won't notice if I sneak off to the bar.

He narrows his eyes at me. "Regardless, I will feel much better knowing you're taken care of tonight."

"Jesus, Jackson. Take off the kid gloves."

He winces. "What is going on with you? Are you trying to start an argument? What did I do to deserve this?"

I blow a hair out of my face. "Nothing. I'm sorry. Maybe a dinner date wasn't the best idea tonight. I'm clearly in a bad mood and I shouldn't be taking it out on you."

"What? I haven't seen you all week." He reaches across the table and begins rubbing his thumb over my hand. "Besides, if Nathan really is gone for the night, there's no reason why we can't go back to my place. It's less than a block away and we haven't been alone in weeks. If you'd agree to move in with me already, we wouldn't have to worry about finding time to be together."

Ugh, not this again. Jackson and I have been seeing each other for two and a half years. I can sense that he's getting frustrated with the plateau we've been on lately. He really has been good to me and Nathan but for some reason I can never get past the dating portion of our relationship. I'm not willing to uproot Nathan from the only home he's ever known unless I know for sure that I have a future with someone. Jackson is a good man, and I care for him, but I don't know if I can see us being together long term. I refuse to examine the reasons behind that right now.

"Please don't do this."

"Do what?" he asks. "Want to take care of you? Love you? God, I'm such a jerk."

I frown. "That's not what I meant. I'm sorry. I really

don't want to argue. Your place tonight sounds nice. Let me just hit the bathroom real quick and then we can go."

He smiles. "I'll take care of the bill and meet you outside."

Okay, I know this is awful, but bathroom was really code for bar. Jackson only has wine at his house and after his drink snatching earlier, I doubt he'll be in any hurry to offer me any. Since becoming a mother, I can count on one hand how many times I've had more than two drinks with dinner, but this week certainly warranted it. I've been working my butt off trying to get this big promotion. As if that wasn't enough, Riley's sudden reappearance is really messing with my head.

I squeeze in between two stools at the crowded bar and signal the bartender. "A double of Maker's Mark, please."

Despite being so busy, he grabs a small glass and pours my drink right away. I down the contents in two gulps and slam the empty on the bar. I dig a twenty out of my purse and place it on the counter.

A large hand slides the bill back to me. "I got this."

I shiver and it's not from the bourbon. That deep voice rolls over me like honey. Always has, whether I want to admit it or not. I look to my left and see Riley grinning at me like an idiot.

"In all the bars, in all the cities, you walk into mine. Two times in one week. Are you following me? Or am I just the luckiest sonofabitch alive?"

I roll my eyes and smile despite my internal refusal to do so. Damn him. "Smooth, Rye. Is that your new pickup line these days?"

"Depends. Is it working?"

I giggle. Giggle! WTH? I blame the alcohol. Finally gathering my proverbial balls, I say, "Thanks for the offer, but I can pay for my own drink. I need to go." I leave the twenty on the bar and turn to walk away.

He grabs my arm. "Devyn, wait."

I glare at him. "I waited for *two years*, Riley. I think that's long enough, don't you?"

He drops my arm. "What? What does that mean?"

I roll my eyes and resume my path to the front door. "Never mind. Forget I said anything."

He follows me. "Never mind, my ass! *What does that mean, Devyn?*"

I finally make it outside and take a deep breath of fresh air. It's pouring rain and I'm getting soaked but I couldn't care less. "It means that I'm done waiting for you, Riley!" I scream. "I'm done waiting for you to grow up and take care of your responsibilities. I'm done pretending that you'll come to your senses one day and realize what you gave up!"

I'm crying hysterically at this point. Again, totally the alcohol's fault. I can't handle my liquor like I used to.

"What?" he shouts. "You're not making any sense!"

"Oh, screw y——"

"Devyn, honey, what's going on?" Jackson steps up to me and holds his umbrella over my head. A little too late, but I appreciate the effort. He looks between me and Riley. "Who's this, babe?"

Riley glares at Jackson. "Who the fuck are you?"

Jackson returns his glare and motions for me to walk away with him. "Come on, honey. Let's get you home."

Riley's mouth drops open. "Devyn, who is this guy?"

I poke him in the chest. "You lost the right to ask five years ago, Riley!" I loop my arm through Jackson's elbow. "Let's go home, *babe*."

I don't risk glancing backwards as we make the short trip to Jackson's building.

NINETEEN

RILEY

WHAT THE MOTHER FUCKITY-FUCK just happened? And who is that asshole taking her *home* with him? I am so goddamn confused, it's not even funny. I watch them walk away while standing here in the downpour like a moron. I wait the entire time for her to look back at me just once but it never happens. They walk to the end of the block and cross the street. I laugh at the absurdity of it all when they step into *my* building. There are way too many coincidences in play here. Takeout forgotten, I give them enough time to get into the elevator before I follow and make my way to my apartment. I stomp through my condo shedding my soaked clothes as I make my way to the liquor cabinet. It's going to be a long night.

DEVYN

. . .

JACKSON HANDS ME A glass of water with some Advil after I step out of the bedroom wearing dry clothes. "I thought you could use this."

I grab the glass and use the water to swallow the pills. "Thanks."

He flips on the fireplace as I take a seat on the leather sectional. "Are you going to tell me what that was all about?"

I sigh. It's bound to come out sooner or later. "That's Riley." I meet his eyes and gulp. "Nathan's father."

Jackson's ears redden. That's his tell when he's irritated. "I see."

Jackson is the only person who knows about my history with Riley. I never mentioned his name because I got so used to avoiding it, but he knows the whole story. He knows how close we were in college, how heartbroken I was when he went to Boston. He also knows how I pined away for almost two years waiting for him to magically show up and tell me that he loves me too. Jackson helped picked up the pieces that Riley left behind.

Shortly before Nathan's second birthday, I had a moment of weakness and called him. Some guy named Dave was the new owner of his phone number. After that, I decided to take the hint and cut my losses. I changed my phone number too and didn't look back. Jackson came into my life shortly thereafter and waited patiently for me to be ready to move on. It took six months before I'd even agree to a single date with him. He's so understanding about everything. He even helps me deal with the guilt that constantly plagues me from not telling Nathan about his dad. Nate's never really asked but I still feel the weight of it as he gets older. He's bound to wonder one of these days.

I groan. "That's all you're going to say?"

He joins me on the couch. "I didn't realize he was in Seattle. When did that happen?"

I shrug. "I don't know. I just discovered it on Monday when I found him hanging out with my brother."

He raises an eyebrow. "You've known since Monday? Well, that explains the whiskey I smell on you."

I hang my head. "Ugh, don't start. Please."

He grabs my hand. "I'm just trying to understand, Devyn. How do you feel about this? How did he take it when you told him about Nathan?"

I swallow hard. "I haven't told him yet. I haven't really had the chance, nor would I even know where to begin."

He squeezes my hand. "What can I do to help?"

I lean my body against his. "You're already doing it, Jackson. I just need time to figure it out. I don't even know how to reach him. I'm going to come clean with Drew and see if I can track him down through him. They seemed to be pretty friendly."

He puts his arm around me. "That sounds like a good starting point. You look exhausted. Why don't we get you into bed?"

"Okay."

TWENTY

RILEY

I'M SITTING AT THE coffee shop across the street nursing a wicked hangover. Last night, I visited with Jack, Jim, and that Dos Equis guy until I passed out on my couch. I haven't drunk like that since college and I'm paying for it.

"Unh," I groan as I thunk my head on the table.

Something starts pulling at my sleeve. "Mister! Hey mister, are you dead or somfin'?"

"No, buddy! Leave that poor man alone."

I look up through slitted eyes and see a little blonde boy standing next to my table. "Oh good, you're awive."

I smirk. "Yep, I sure am."

A woman runs over to him and grabs his arm. "I'm so sorry; he has no sense of personal space." I meet her eyes and she glares. "You! I take back my apology. I don't say sorry to assholes."

It's the redhead from Monday night that came into the bar with Devyn. "Rainey, is it? Nice to see you again."

135

"Uh huh," she scoffs.

"Why is he an ath-hole, Aunt Wainey?"

She gasps. "Shh! Don't say asshole. Your mom will kill me!"

I laugh and give the foul-mouthed little boy a good once over. So this must be Devyn's son. He's a cute little guy.

"Hey, mister, you have holes in your cheeks like I do!"

Huh? Holes in my cheeks? Oh, he must mean my dimples. I study his face more carefully. He has his mommy's hair but that's where the resemblance ends. He has big brown eyes, a medium complexion, and yep, two giant dimples just like me. "Yep, buddy, I sure do. Trust me, they'll come in handy later in life. The ladies love 'em."

Rainey rolls her eyes. "Nice. Any more lessons in woman-izing you'd like to give today?"

"What's womanizing?" the boy asks.

"Shit!" Rainey says under her breath. "Don't repeat that either, Nathan."

I crouch down on the floor so I can be eye level with him. "Hey, Nathan, do you like chocolate milk? Would you like me to get you one?"

He does a fist pump in the air. "Yes! I LOVE choc-wit milk!"

I stand up. "One choc-wit milk coming right up."

"No, really you don't—" Rainey says.

I pick up the carton from the refrigerated case and hand it to the cashier. "Too late."

I poke the little straw through the top and hand it to him. "Here you go, buddy."

Nathan climbs up and sits on the chair at my table. "Thanks duth-bag."

"Nathan!" Rainey scolds.

I laugh. "Did he just call me a douchebag?"

She bites her lip. "He sure did. We're working on

extracting Uncle Drew's potty mouth from his vocabulary. It's a daily struggle."

I gesture for her to take a seat. "Care to join us?"

She begrudgingly sits down and takes a sip of her coffee. "Don't think this means I'm okay with the stunt you pulled the other day."

I hold my hands up and take the chair next to Nathan. "Don't worry, I'll pretend you're dying to kick me in the nuts."

"No pretending necessary," she mutters.

"Uh oh, should I go back home and get my cup?" I joke.

She raises her eyes and smirks. "I'll control myself for the kid's sake."

Nathan puts his little hand on my cheek. "Hey, mister, you have brown eyes like me too. Mommy says they look like choc-wit pools of yummy-ness."

This kid is a riot. I glance over at Rainey while I laugh again. She's staring at our exchange, completely frozen.

"Holy shit," she whispers.

"What's wrong?" I ask.

She slams her hand over her mouth. "Oh my God, we have to go. She stands up and quickly scoops Nathan into her arms. Come on dude, we have to go get mommy."

"But mommy's posta' meet us here!" he whines. "I want my choc-wit milk, Aunt Wainey!"

What the hell is going on? I look at them trying to figure out what's making her freak out so suddenly. I look at Nathan again as he's squirming in her arms. His eyes are starting to water, totally tugging on my heart strings. Oh fuck, his *big brown eyes*. His dimples. His skin tone. I think I'm a little slow from the hangover but there's no denying the fact that I'm staring at a living picture of my four-year-old self.

"Holy shit," I echo.

. . .

DEVYN

I WALK INTO THE coffee shop across the street from Jackson's condo. Rainey is towards the back holding a squirming Nathan in her arms. She's talking to some guy as she spots me and gives me a panicked look. Nathan sees me at the same time and she sets him down so he can run up to me.

"Mommy!"

I pull him into a hug. "Hey, big guy! Did you have fun at the zoo this morning?"

"I did!" he says excitedly. "I got to see hippos, lions, and a bunch of monkeys that were dancing all funny!"

I laugh. "Dancing monkeys?"

Rainey joins us. "Yeah, they were *dancing*. You know how monkeys like to *dance* a lot?"

Humping monkeys. Got it. "Ah, *dancing*. Yeah, that's really cool, bud. What else did you see?"

"I saw—"

"Devyn, we need to have a *big* talk," a deep voice interrupts.

I look away from my son who's still talking up a storm. My jaw drops when I see his furious father standing right behind Lorraine. "Aw, crap."

TWENTY-ONE

DEVYN

RAINEY GRABS NATHAN'S HAND. "Hey, buddy, can I ask you a favor?"

Nathan looks up to her. "Whatcha want, Aunt Wainey?"

"Do you think it'd be okay if we went for ice cream and then I can drive you home afterwards? I'm really craving some mint chocolate chip and I think Mommy and her friend here need to have some grownup talk."

Nathan tugs on my capris. "Momma, can I? Can I? I want some ice cweam!"

I ruffle his hair. "Sure, buddy. That would be fine." I mouth *thank you* to Rainey.

She nods as she leads Nate out the door.

Riley waits for them to round the corner before saying, "Let's go back to my place. I don't think a public venue is the right place to have this conversation."

"Do you live nearby?"

He tilts his head towards Jackson's condo building. "Right across the street."

My eyes bulge. "Across the street? Like, *right* across the street? The red brick building?"

Riley laughs sardonically. "Yep. I believe you're familiar with it."

I gulp. "Yeah, I am."

He jerks his head. "Follow me."

My eyes wander throughout the lobby looking for any sign of Jackson. I'm not trying to hide the fact that I'm going to Riley's…I'll tell him. I just don't want to run into him right now because it would exacerbate the already tense situation. I relax marginally when we step inside the elevator and he presses the button for the third floor, two levels down from Jackson's unit.

There's no way he hasn't put the pieces of Nathan's paternity together. Nate is Riley's little mini me. It would only take a matter of seconds for him to see that, I'm sure. He doesn't say a word as we ride the elevator to his floor and walk down the hallway. I have no idea what he's thinking. He's obviously angry but is that because he feels cheated out of knowing his son? Or because he *has* a son and doesn't want to be shackled down? Will he want to be a part of Nate's life?

Riley digs into his pocket and produces a set of keys. He unlocks the door and pushes it open, stepping aside to let me in. The layout of his condo is pretty similar to Jackson's. There's a small kitchen with a large island to the left and a living/dining room combo immediately off the entryway. The space is tidy for the most part with the exception of several empty liquor bottles on the counter. Geez, that's a lot of alcohol. Has Riley become a heavy drinker? I raise an eyebrow as I wonder but say nothing.

. . .

RILEY

DEVYN IS EYEING THE empty bottles of liquor in my kitchen. What gives her the right to judge me for having a rough night when she's been hiding my *son* from me? For almost five years! What possible reason could she have for doing something so fucking selfish?

I still haven't said a word at this point and I can tell that it's making her nervous. Good.

She nods towards the couch. "Do you mind if I take a seat for this?"

I cross my arms. "By all means, make yourself comfortable."

She winces. Probably from the tone in my voice that says I want her to be anything *but* comfortable right now. Remaining completely silent, I continue staring her down.

She slinks down into the cushions and sighs. "Please say something."

"I'm pretty sure you don't want to hear what I'm thinking right now," I scoff. "It's probably better if you start."

"Ugh, I really should've grabbed a coffee first," she groans.

I storm over to her and shove my cup from the coffee house into her hand. I'm towering over her right now and I'm irritated at how badly I want to take her into my arms. I angrily step back and sit on a barstool across the room.

"Talk, Devyn."

TWENTY-TWO

RILEY

SHE TAKES A SIP of my coffee. "You still drink mochas, huh?"

I scrub my hand over my stubbled jaw. "I wasn't talking about the fucking coffee, Devyn. Help me understand why in the hell you thought it would be a good idea to hide the fact that we have a *child* together."

She takes a deep breath. "I called you as soon as I found out. You were too busy plying some girl with drinks to answer."

I think about that for a minute. Oh hell, she must be talking about the time that annoying girl answered my phone in Boston. "Jesus, Devyn. One phone call? You didn't think something like this was important enough to try again?"

She juts her chin out and glares at me. *Fucking glares!* "Not *one* phone call, Riley. *Twelve!* Eleven phone calls *and* countless text messages after our night in the hotel. And another attempt almost two years later but you had changed your phone number. It was pretty clear you had no interest in speaking with me."

I run my hand over my head. "That's what this is about? I was a stupid kid! You should have tried harder."

She stands up and flings her arms out, spraying coffee all over the hardwood floors. "That's my point, Riley! I was *having a kid*! I didn't have the luxury of indulging a *grown man* who couldn't pull his head out of his ass and see what was right in front of him! I didn't have time to try harder! I had seven months to figure out a new plan in life. It wasn't just me anymore. I had another human being that I was going to be responsible for. I needed to focus on that, not trying to make you talk to me."

"You still should have told me," I grumble.

She sits back down and hangs her head in her hands. "Yeah, maybe I should have. But I was scared. And heartbroken. And hormonal. That's not exactly a good recipe for rational thought."

One word sticks out. "Heartbroken?"

She lifts her head and rolls her eyes. "Oh please, Rye. Are you really going to make me say it?"

I walk towards her and sit on the edge of the coffee table. She shivers when our knees touch. "Say what?"

She stares at her hands. "That night...it meant something to me. I know that wasn't part of the deal, but I *know* you felt it too. For whatever reason, you obviously weren't willing to acknowledge it and that hurt. After everything we'd been through...we knew each other better than anyone, yet you chose to run. It *hurt*."

Every bit of anger I had inside of me melts. I lift her chin with my finger. "I was a coward."

She laughs mirthlessly. "You think?"

Tears are forming in her eyes and it's killing me. I lean in closer. "Devyn, I—"

Her phone rings, startling us both. She pulls it out of her purse and I can see that the asshole from last night is calling.

She scoots away from me and slides her finger across the screen to answer. "Hi." She turns her head away as she listens to whatever the fuck he's saying. She lowers her voice. "No, there's been a slight change in plans."

I tune out their conversation as I feel my face getting red. I know I have no right to be jealous but that doesn't stop me from feeling it. I can't stop thinking about the smug look on his face when he took her in his arm and walked away. He said he was taking her *home* which implies familiarity. I don't like it. Not one bit.

Devyn glances at me over her shoulder. "Mmm hmm. You too. Bye, Jackson."

You too? Did she just tell him that she loved him? Oh Christ, this situation is shittier than I thought.

DEVYN

THANK GOD JACKSON CALLED when he did. I'm pretty sure Riley was about to kiss me. And I honestly don't know how I would've responded to that. Hearing Jackson's voice helped bring me back into the present. Riley is my past. I simply got caught up in my emotions talking about it with him.

"Riley, I have to get going."

He frowns. "Back to Jackson?"

I bite my lip. "Not that it's any of your business, but no. I need to get home to Nathan."

"What's the story with you and that guy?"

"Jackson?"

"No, the fucking Dalai Lama."

147

I glare. "You don't need to be so rude."

"Answer the question, Dev."

"I really don't think that's any of your business."

"Of course it's my business!" he shouts. "If this guy is going to be spending time around *my son*, I have the right to know."

I clench my fists. "He's been spending time with *our son* for over two years! Are you saying you don't trust my judgment?"

He stiffens. "Give me your phone."

What? Is he going to call Jackson? "No."

He rolls his eyes. "I'm not going to do anything stupid, Devyn. I want to program my number into it."

I hand it to him hesitantly. I watch as he opens the text window and types something real quick before hitting send. His phone beeps a second later.

He pulls it out of his pocket and looks at the display. "There. Now we both know how to reach each other. And for the record, I changed my number when I moved to Georgia. I had planned on settling there and wanted a local number. It had nothing to do with running away."

"You lived in Georgia? When?"

"After grad school," he replies. "I took a job in Savannah designing private aircrafts."

"Oh," I whisper. "Then why are you in Seattle?"

He gulps. "That's a story for another day. You need to get home, remember?"

I stand and walk to the door. "Yeah, I do."

He follows me and opens the door. As I step into the hallway he says, "Dev, we'll figure this out, okay? I'm not going anywhere."

I nod. "Okay."

TWENTY-THREE

RILEY

SHE'S BEEN WITH HIM for over *two years*? Shit. This definitely throws a wrench in my get Devyn back plans. Drew said she's not living with him so they're obviously not that serious, but still. I grit my teeth when I think about where she spent the night last night. Now I *really* don't like the guy. I need to figure out exactly where they stand so I can plan my next move. I may have been a total man slut back in the day but I would never condone cheating. I've always thought that if you're unhappy enough to even *think* about cheating, you need to figure your shit out or leave the relationship. Besides, I wouldn't dream of sharing Devyn once I finally had her. No fucking way.

I pick up my phone and dial Brody as something comes to mind.

"Hey, asshole! Are you done unpacking yet?"

"Almost," I say. "I still have to hang photos and shit but

other than that, I'm done. Are you planning to watch the games tomorrow?"

"Do you have to ask? What's up? You wanna hang?"

"My satellite isn't hooked up yet so I was hoping I could tag along with you. Maybe you could see what Drew and his sister are up to and ask them to join us?"

Brody laughs. "Ah, I get it now. Well, lucky for you my plans happen to include hanging out at Drew's house. I'm sure he won't mind an extra guest. The hot sister should be there for your viewing pleasure."

"What? I don't want to see the sister! I'm just looking for a place to watch football."

"Right, buddy. Are you in, or what?"

I smile. "Yeah, I'm definitely in."

DEVYN

I'M JUST ABOUT TO walk out the door when Drew says, "Hey, a couple of the guys are coming over to hang for the games. They should be here in about an hour. Will you grab some extra chips and beer while you're at the store?"

I freeze with my hand on the doorknob. "*Which* couple of guys?"

"My friend Brody and that guy you knew in college."

"Riley?" I shriek.

"Yeah. Why? Is that not okay? I know he was kind of a dick but he promised me he'd behave next time he saw you."

I look down at the faded sweatpants and threadbare 49ers t-shirt I'm wearing. "Drew! Why didn't you tell me earlier? We can't have people over when I look like this! I don't have time to get ready *and* shop for groceries!"

He gives me a fleeting glance. "Who cares what you're wearing?"

I groan and look down the hall to make sure Nathan is still playing in his room. "Drew, there's something you need to know about Riley."

"What?"

I blow a hair out of my face. "Well, there's no good way to say it. Other than to come straight out with it I guess."

He scrunches his face. "What the fuck are you rambling about?"

I take a deep breath and exhale. "Riley is Voldemort."

"What does Harry Potter have to do with this? You're not making any sense."

I roll my eyes. "Think about that for a second. Riley is *he who must not be named*." I give him a few seconds but he still looks lost. "Oh God, fine! Riley is Nathan's *father*. Is that clear enough?"

"What.The.Fuck. Are you shitting me right now?" he bellows.

"Keep your voice down!" I whisper-shout. "Nathan doesn't know yet. And I just told Riley yesterday."

"Yesterday? You saw him? Where? And what do you mean you just told him *yesterday*? I thought he walked when he found out you were pregnant!"

"At the coffee shop across from Jackson's house. He and Riley apparently live in the same building. And I didn't exactly get the chance to tell him I was pregnant. We never even dated. We were friends...and we hooked up one night. He didn't know I ever had a child until *you* told him."

Drew laughs. "Oh, this is fucking priceless. Does Jackson know?"

"Yes, Jackson knows. Well, about the paternity thing. Not that they both live at the Marselle."

"So what the hell are you going to do? Am I supposed to pretend I don't know?"

"No, you don't need to pretend. Lorraine knows too. Just don't be open about it with everyone until we've figured out how to tell Nathan. I just need a little time."

Drew stands up and grabs his keys off the kitchen counter. "Go do whatever girly shit you need to do. I'll go to the store."

I smile and kiss him on the cheek. "Have I told you lately that you're the best big brother ever?"

"Yeah, yeah," he mutters.

TWENTY-FOUR

RILEY

I'M SITTING AGAINST THE curb in front of Devyn's building waiting for Brody to get here. I pull up my text messages and smile while reading the one that I sent from her phone to mine.

Devyn: My memory didn't do your hotness justice. The real thing is SO much better.

It was my attempt at lightening the mood. I was pissed and reacted poorly when I found out about Nathan. I felt a reminder of how playful we could be together was in order. Did Drew tell her I was coming over? I don't want her to be blindsided so I type a quick message.

Me: Hey, did Drew give you the heads up that you're having company for the game today? And by company, I mean ME and Brody. Are you okay with that?

I wait for her reply.

Devyn: He did tell me.

That's it? Really? I'm staring at my screen, waiting for

that little bubble to pop up indicating she was typing some-thing else. Hmm.

I start typing again when nothing comes.

Me: And? Are you okay with that?

The typing bubble is there but no message comes. I wait for three minutes. She's either writing a novel or is thinking about her reply very carefully. I'd bet on the latter. Finally, she hits send.

Devyn: Yes I'm okay with that. Nathan is here though. We need to tread lightly until we have a chance to discuss how to tell him. Agree?

I smile, thankful she doesn't tell me to turn around and go home.

Me: Agreed.

I look at the time and realize Brody is late. I don't want to wait anymore; I'm anxious to see my girl. And my boy.

I send one last message.

Me: I'm in front of your building. Brody isn't here yet but I'd like to come up if that's okay.

Devyn: Okay.

She doesn't need to tell me twice. I get out of my car and run up to her front door.

DEVYN

I'M STARING AT RILEY'S text trying not to show my anxiety. I scroll up and read through our conversation. I laugh when I read his first message while we were exchanging phone numbers. I didn't catch it before.

"What's so funny, Momma?" Nathan asks.

I lock my phone and place it on the end table. "Oh, nothing, baby. I just read something funny."

Drew looks at me suspiciously but doesn't say anything.

The buzzer sounds, indicating Riley's arrival. Drew gets up from the couch to answer it. "Yeah?"

"Hi, it's Riley."

Drew buzzes him in and gives me a look that says, *Are you ready for this?*

I nod in silent acknowledgment.

TWENTY-FIVE

RILEY

I KNOCK ON THE door, trying not to reveal how anxious I am. The door opens a crack and Drew fills the space. Why does he look so homicidal?

"Oh, hey, Dr—"

Drew flattens his palm on my chest and walks me backwards, shutting the door behind him. He doesn't stop until I'm against the wall.

He takes a half step back but still looks like he's going to kill me. "Listen, asshole. Devyn told me who you are. Who you *really* are."

I hold my hands up. "Did she also tell you that I didn't know? I would've never stayed away if I knew she was pregnant."

He runs a hand through his hair and starts pacing. "Yeah, she told me that part too. But the fact remains that you *broke her.* She was one of the strongest people I knew ever since she was a little girl. When our mom got sick—when she

161

died—Devyn was only ten years old but she somehow became the glue that held our family together. And when our dad followed, she was still rock solid and stoic as ever.

"When you...when she became pregnant with Nathan... she became a shell of her former self. Sure, she put on a brave face, but when she didn't think I was looking, I saw how devastated she was. It took her *years* before she slowly started coming back to life. And I may not exactly like the guy she's with now, but he's good to her and he's good to the kid. If she chooses to stay with him, you stay the fuck out of the way. You *will not* cause her any more grief or you'll be answering to me." He takes a fist full of my shirt and leans into me. "Capiche?"

I gulp. "Yep."

DEVYN

I'M PLAYING WITH THE hem of my t-shirt waiting for Drew and Riley to come through the door. What the heck is going on out there? Drew's an extraordinarily big guy; therefore, he intimidates people pretty easily if you don't know what a teddy bear he is. He's probably using that to his advantage right now and playing the big brother card, trying to scare the crap out of Riley.

"Where'd Unca' Drew go?" Nathan asks.

I get up from the couch and start walking towards the door. "He just stepped into the hall for a second, buddy. I'll go get him."

I open the door and peek my head out. Riley is standing against the wall and Drew is directly in front of him puffing his chest out. Yep, he's definitely doing the *don't you dare hurt my sister or I'll break your face* crap.

Drew sees me, takes a step back, and smiles. "Hey, sis! Riley and I were just having a little guy talk."

"Uh huh," I mutter.

Riley looks my way and smiles. "Hi."

I return his grin. "Hi."

Drew looks between us and rolls his eyes. "Uh, yeah. I'm going inside." He looks to me. "You coming?"

I look at Riley. "We'll be there in a minute. Distract Nate for me?"

Drew scowls and steps past me. "Yeah, yeah. Don't forget what I said, Riley."

I wait for the door to close before speaking. "Was he giving you the big brother speech?"

Riley grimaces. "You could say that." He gives me a good once over and his eyes light up. Stepping forward, he grabs the hem of my shirt and says, "You still have it."

I shiver when the tip of his finger brushes against my bare skin. "It's my lucky shirt. They win every time I wear it."

He smiles. "So I've heard."

I'd kept my old 49ers shirt on but exchanged my baggy sweatpants for a more flattering pair of yoga capris. I wasn't going to dress up since we're just watching football but I don't want to look scrappy if *anyone* comes over. My only real concession is a bit of pink lip gloss.

He continues running his finger against the seam, staring at the sliver of skin he's exposed. I know I should probably step out of his reach but my feet are rooted firmly in place.

He clears his throat. "So, Nathan's in there?"

I nod. "He is."

He scrunches his face. "Is *Jackson* in there?"

"No, Jackson isn't really a sports fan."

Riley looks perplexed. "How is that even possible?"

I shrug. "I don't know. He was never really exposed as a kid, I guess. It's not a big deal."

"Are you serious?" he asks incredulously. "You love sports year round. How can you be with someone who doesn't share something that takes up so much of your time?"

I take a moment to remind myself that Riley hasn't been an active parent yet. "Yeah, I do love a good game, but it's not the same anymore. I catch them when I can, but Nathan and my job take up most of my time now. If I do want to hang with the group and watch something, Jackson doesn't mind. He'd rather do his own thing than suffer through something that doesn't interest him."

Riley opens his mouth to say something but the elevator dings, indicating a stop on my floor. I see Brody step out and start walking our way.

He nods when he sees us. "Hey, cocksucker, I thought you were going to wait for me outside?"

Riley turns towards him. "That was before you were late, asshat."

Brody laughs and then zeros in on Riley's hand which is now gripping my waist. I follow his gaze and immediately step back so Riley's hand falls to his side.

I rub the back of my neck and open the door. "C'mon in, guys."

RILEY

SHIT, I CAN'T BELIEVE Brody just walked in on that. The touch was purely innocent. Okay, *mostly* innocent, but I know he picked up on the tension in the air. I have no doubt he's going to grill me about it later. I can't stop thinking about what Drew said. I do need to watch myself. Devyn is involved with someone and I need to respect that, despite my suspicions that they have very little in common. It's just so damn hard when I feel so comfortable around her even after all these years apart. I touched her countless times during our friendship —it's second nature almost. Sure, being together that one night changed that—it's much more sexually charged now—but it still feels like the natural thing to do.

We follow Devyn inside. The place is nice. Homey. The walls are light gray with large windows overlooking the city. Their living room is right off the entryway and the attached kitchen is towards the back. Framed photos are everywhere but I can't really make them out without looking too obvious. I make a mental note to look later.

Drew gets up from the leather recliner and greets Brody with a man hug/shake thing. "Hey, dude, how's it hangin'?"

"Down to my knees, brother. Down to my knees," Brody replies.

Drew laughs. "In your dreams maybe."

Devyn rolls her eyes and takes the chair Drew had just vacated. Nathan immediately climbs on her lap and starts shoveling orange crackers into his mouth.

I kneel in front of them. "Hey, buddy."

Nathan grabs a handful of little orange fish from his bowl. "Hey, dickweed."

"Nathan!" Devyn scolds.

Drew laughs. "That's my little man." He leans over the arm of the couch and gives Nathan a fist bump.

Devyn glares at Drew. "You're not helping. Go put money in the jar."

Drew groans and starts walking towards the kitchen.

"The jar?" I ask.

Devyn smirks. "Yeah, Drew is single-handedly funding Nathan's college education. Every time he *or* Nate say a bad word, he has to pay up. We all know the kid didn't get that part of his vocabulary from me."

I laugh. "I guess I'm going to have to watch what I say in certain company, huh?"

"Yeah, keep laughing, asshole," Drew says. "You just wait."

"Unca' Drew! Add another dollar!" Nathan says excitedly.

"Damn it!" Drew shouts.

Brody cracks up. "There goes another one."

Drew mutters something under his breath as he digs out his wallet and shoves several bills into the jar. "Consider this a deposit. I have a feeling I'm going to earn it today."

TWENTY-SIX

DEVYN

BRODY LEFT BEFORE THE night game saying he had to collect on a bet but Riley stayed through all three. I'm internally freaking out about how easy it is being with him. Watching him interact with our son is so much better than I had imagined. Who knew he'd be such a natural with kids?

Nate clung to him the whole day, hanging on every word. I wonder if he can sense something. One thing that I've learned as a parent is how intuitive kids can be. Nate blows my mind constantly. Speaking of mind-blowing, Riley has me floored when it's time to put Nathan to bed.

"Can I do it?" he asks.

I crinkle my brows. "Do what?"

"Put him to bed." He ruffles Nate's hair. "Would you like that, buddy?"

Nathan pumps his fist in the air. "Heck yes!" He tugs on my pants. "Momma, is that okay? Please?" He extends the last word.

I smile. "Sure, honey. Why don't you go pick out a book and Riley will be there in a minute?"

Nathan bounces down the hall into his room.

Riley grabs my hand. "Thank you."

I stare at our joined hands. "Um, yeah. Sure."

We stand there in silence looking at each other.

Drew gets up from the couch and stretches. "Yeah...so I have to be on shift early tomorrow so I'm going to bed too. You kids have fun. Don't do anything I would do."

Riley smirks as Drew closes the door to his bedroom. "Doesn't he mean don't do anything I *wouldn't* do?"

I chuckle. "No, I'm pretty sure he said what he meant. Don't get me wrong...Drew's incredible; he saved me when I didn't have anyone." I shift on my feet as I catch his somber expression from my comment. "Anyway, he's really just a big kid at heart. He definitely doesn't act his age most days."

Riley tugs on my hand and pulls me in for a hug. "Hey, I don't think apologizing for everything is even close to adequate, but you know that I wish I were there, right? Through everything? I don't think I could ever regret anything more in my life."

Tears form in my eyes. God, I missed this. "Riley, I—"

"Eeeewwww!" Nathan says. "Are you guys going to make a baby or somfin'?"

"What?" we both ask as we break apart.

"Christopher says that babies get in their mommy's tummies when grownups hug."

Riley raises his eyebrows. "Who's this Christopher kid?"

I laugh. "A friend of his at preschool." I kneel down to Nathan's level. "Honey, you see me hugging other grownups all the time. That's not where babies come from."

"Well then how do you make 'em?" he asks.

"Isn't this conversation supposed to happen much later?" Riley mutters.

I kiss Nathan on the cheek. "I'll tell you when you're a little older."

"Aw, mom!" Nathan whines.

I laugh as I stand up and look at Riley. "He's all yours. Good luck with that."

Riley takes Nate's hand and starts walking down the hall. Nathan continues asking about the birds and bees and Riley looks petrified as he dodges each question. He casts a backwards glance as they step into the bedroom. I give him a thumbs-up and a smile as he mouths, *Help*.

TWENTY-SEVEN

RILEY

I PLOP DOWN ON the couch next to Devyn about forty-five minutes later. "I can't believe you just threw me to the wolves like that!"

She laughs. "Oh please! That's not the worst he's ever given me. You should've been there when he asked, 'Mom, why does my wiener get big when I touch it a bunch?'"

My eyes widen. "What? He gets *boners*?"

"Yep. Playing with his junk is his new obsession. It's totally normal at this age. Kids are curious. He doesn't really understand what he's doing."

My jaw drops. "How do I not know this? I'm a guy! I don't remember being obsessed with my junk until I was at least thirteen."

She starts laughing so hard tears are coming out of her eyes. God, she's beautiful. "You're obsessed with your junk, huh?"

"What? No, that's not what I meant," I smirk. "These

days, I'm much more obsessed with boobs. Come to think of it, it was pretty much the same back then too."

She looks down at her chest. "Yeah, well, sorry I don't really have the goods to help you out there."

I follow her gaze. "Boobs are boobs, Devyn. Big or small, I love them all."

She looks up and catches me staring at her chest. "Yeah, right. That's what every guy says when he gets stuck with someone who has small boobs. I know you all really wish we looked like porn stars."

I clench my jaw. It pisses me off that she still has these insecurities. If Jackson were a real man, he would've squashed them by now. I lean forward and look directly in her eyes to punctuate my next words. "Are you really doubting me? Do I need to prove it, Devyn? Say the word and I'll make sure you have *no question* about it."

DEVYN

"SAY THE WORD AND I'll make sure you have no question about it," Riley says.

Oh God, why did he have to say that? Now all I can think about are unbidden images of me and Riley together. Naked and sweaty —in all sorts of compromising positions. The sexual tension in the air is palpable. I think I groan. I've never felt something this electric with anyone but him. Jackson's the only other man I've slept with, but I dated other guys before. The chemistry was never even close to what Riley and I have. Sadly, not even with Jackson. Sure, I'm attracted to him, and our sex is…good. But with Riley, I could practically orgasm just hearing his voice. I feel like some sex-starved demon possesses my body right now.

I take a few deep breaths before replying, "Riley, I think it's time for you to go home."

He blinks a few times. "Is that what you really want?"

Yes. No. Ugh, I don't know.

I close my eyes. "It's the right thing to do."

"Devyn, look at me."

My eyes snap open. "What do you want me to say here, Riley?"

"I want the truth. Do you really think I can't feel how much you want me right now? Do you *really* want me to leave?"

I steel my resolve to do the right thing and not be ruled by my stupid hormones. "Yes, I really want you to leave."

His jaw tics as he stands up. "Fine. Go ahead and lie to yourself if it makes you feel better." He walks to the front door and opens it. Before leaving he adds, "But Devyn, you and I both know that won't last long. You need to think long and hard about what you're going to do about it. I think you know me well enough to know where I stand on the subject. And if there's any confusion, I'd be happy to clear it up. Just say the word."

TWENTY-EIGHT

RILEY

I CAN'T BELIEVE ANOTHER work week is ending. I haven't seen Devyn in almost two weeks mainly because we've both been working such crazy hours. We've talked every night about the daily minutia of our lives but mostly about Nathan. She's sent me dozens of pictures, told me stories about his childhood, her pregnancy, all the stuff I've missed out on. It still kills me that I wasn't there but I love hearing about everything from her point of view. She's so animated when she talks about our son. Hearing her laugh about something totally inappropriate he said during the day is priceless. I've tried shifting the subject, dying to get more information about her relationship with Jackson, or how she feels about the possibility of us, but she shuts me down every damn time. I'm so desperate to hear anything and everything about Nathan though that I let her.

We decided that we're going to break the news to him slowly by scheduling family outings. I smile when I think about that. I have a family of my own. It's not just me and my folks anymore. Speaking of, they took the news much better than I expected. I took full blame for the situation. I wanted to make sure they never faulted Devyn for her actions. We both made shitty decisions back then but it was ultimately my pushing her away that created the domino effect. They're flying up next week to meet the two people I love more than anything and I can't wait to show them off.

It's been tough putting any plans into action so far because Dev's been working twelve hour days, six days a week. She normally does the nine-to-five thing but she's trying to nab a big client so she can get promoted. Her pitch is next week and she promised we'll schedule something afterwards. I Googled kids' activities around Seattle and already have a huge list of things I want to do with them.

My phone vibrates in my pocket and I smile when I see her name on the display. "Hi there."

"Hi. How was your day?"

"Good," I reply while moving throughout my condo switching off lights. "I have news."

"Yeah?"

I slip out of my jeans and climb into bed. "Yep. I made an offer on a house today."

"You what?" she shrieked. "Didn't you just buy the condo?"

"Nah, it's a rental. I didn't want to buy anything until I knew where I'd be settling down."

"I'm confused."

I laugh. "Well, you see…there's this girl that I thought was living in Portland. Seattle is the closest place where I could become gainfully employed but I planned on commuting if need be. I was originally looking at real estate halfway in between. Turns out, Seattle's where I'm supposed to be."

She's silent for a moment. "Riley…"

"Yeah, baby?"

She blows out a breath. "I don't know what to say to that. Jackson and I—"

I groan. "Can we please not put a damper on my big, exciting news? I'm not going to lie. I want both of you there with me. Of course I do. But I'm not asking you to commit to anything, Devyn. You should definitely know that Nathan will have his own bedroom though. And a big backyard. Maybe even a dog."

"A dog, huh? What if I told you he's more of a cat person?" I swear I can hear her smiling through the phone.

"Pft, he's my boy. There's no way he's a cat person."

She laughs. "So, where's this house at?"

"Mercer Island. My realtor said it has one of the best school districts in the area. I made that my top priority when we were searching since Nate will be starting kindergarten soon."

She gasps. "You're really in for the long haul with this parenthood thing, aren't you?"

I smile. "Balls to the wall, baby."

DEVYN

HE BOUGHT A HOUSE? In an incredible family friendly area no less? What am I supposed to do with that information? I've intentionally avoided discussing my relationship status with Jackson but Riley's spiel about school districts makes me realize that he never considered the possibility that I wouldn't be with him. Nate can't attend school in Mercer Island and live with me in Belltown. Riley wants the whole package and nothing less.

My hands are shaking so bad I'm having trouble holding the phone to my ear. I don't know if it's from excitement or trepidation. "So when do I get to see this fancy new house?"

"Well, I don't close until the fifteenth but we can do a drive by anytime you want. I can always call the realtor and make an appointment if you want to see the inside too."

I smile thinking about showing Nathan where his new bedroom will be. "That'd be nice, Rye. Why don't we plan that as one of our outings?"

"You've got a deal, Dev."

TWENTY-NINE

RILEY

BRODY EYES ME CAREFULLY. "So…Devyn, huh?"

I take a sip of beer, trying to figure out where he's going with this. "What about her?"

He shoves a french fry in his mouth. "Fuck, dude. Give me a little credit. I'm not blind."

I stare at the wall of TV screens. Several college games are showing but I stopped paying attention when he mentioned Devyn's name. "Blind?"

He flips me off. "Don't treat me like I'm an idiot, asshole. I'm talking about the fact that Devyn's kid looks exactly like you. I always thought he looked familiar but I didn't put it together until I saw the two of you in the same room. And not only do you have a kid that you failed to mention, but Drew's hot sister is the goddamn magic pussy you've been obsessing over the entire time I've known you. What are the odds, man?"

"For the record, I didn't know about Nathan until I came here."

He raises his eyebrows. "No shit?"

I nod. "No shit. But what makes you think Devyn is the girl I've been talking about?"

He rolls his eyes. "Because *I have eyes*, douchebag."

I cross my arms over my chest. "Care to explain?"

"Hmm…let's see." He holds up his index finger. "First of all, you look at her like she's a walking wet dream. I know she's hot, dude, like *really hot*, but your look says that you don't need to *imagine* undressing her because you already *know* what's underneath the clothes. Which makes sense I suppose since you made a baby, but this is more. It's like she's your personal goddess or something."

Yeah, that's about right. I didn't realize I was being so obvious about it. Damn it!

"And second of all?" I ask.

He holds up a second finger. "Secondly, she looks at *you* like you hung the fucking moon or something."

"She does?"

His eye roll is even more exaggerated this time. "Yes, dumbfuck, she does. The rest wasn't too hard to put together. There's an obvious familiarity between you two. And it's more than two people who got naked once upon a time. You told me that the M.P. was your best friend throughout your first four years in college. Your comfort level with her matches that. The fact that Drew looked like he was severely constipated the other Sunday helped too. I just did the math and it all added up."

"Maybe he *was* constipated?"

He laughs. "Did you miss the part where he disappeared for twenty minutes saying he had to 'drop the kids off at the pool'?"

"Nope," I say. "Because that's when Nathan said, 'Uncle

Drew, don't you mean you're going to make a chocolate sundae for the sewer monster?'"

Brody is cracking up at this point. "Man, I love that kid!"

I smile. "He's pretty great, isn't he?"

He gives me a serious look. "What are you going to do, man? You know she's got a boyfriend, right? She's been with the guy forever."

I turn my hat around so the bill is facing backwards. "I don't know. I really don't know."

"Hey guys." I look to my left and see Devyn's friend, Rainey.

She motions for Brody to move over. "Mind if I join you?"

He slides over in the booth to make room. "What are you doing here, Rainey?"

She shrugs. "I felt like playing darts and having a couple of beers."

Brody raises his eyebrows. "By yourself?"

"I never have trouble finding someone to play," she says. "Or someone to buy me drinks, for that matter."

Brody glares at her. "Is that so?"

She holds up her bottle and nods to a guy over by the bar. "I certainly didn't pay for this. He did."

Brody takes a long pull from his bottle while he's glaring holes through the guy at the bar. That's an...*interesting* reaction.

Rainey diverts her eyes to me. "So, Riley...what were you boys talking about before I got here?"

"Uh..." I stammer.

"How he's going to get Devyn to break up with her boyfriend," Brody interrupts.

She smirks. "You don't say."

I flip Brody off. "No, I don't say. I mean...I *didn't* say that. I said I don't know what I'm going to do about her."

"But you want her to leave Jackson, right? To be with you?" she asks. "She told me about the house."

"Well…yeah," I reply.

She smiles. "Look, Riley. I'm going to tell you something but if you mention anything about it to Devyn, I will castrate you."

My balls instinctively recoil into my body. "What's that?"

"I'm on your side."

"Come again?"

"Jackson's…decent enough. He's good to her. And Nathan. But she's different since you've moved to town. She lights up whenever she talks about you. And I know now that you didn't know about the kid. I still think you're an asshole for what you did to her, but I get your side of it too."

"She talks about me?"

"Of course she talks about you, dipshit. I'm her best friend. And you're her child's father, who has magically reappeared."

"Wow, you don't mince words, do you?" I mutter.

"Quit being such a Sensitive Sally," she says. "Geez, no wonder you and Brody are friends. You're both whiny little bitches."

"Hey!" Brody complains.

She rolls her eyes and ignores him. "My point was that I think you're a better fit for her. And not just because you can clearly incinerate her panties with a simple glance. I've never seen her react to someone like she does with you. It's refreshing to see her so…alive. And since you're the kid's father…even better. You can be the picture perfect family that she's always dreamed of having for Nathan. But she needs to settle things with Jackson on her own terms. And if by chance she chooses to stay with him, I'm going to support her then too. Whatever decision she makes, you need to respect that as well."

"Yeah, easy for you to say," I scoff. "She and my son mean *everything* to me. I'm not going to give that up without a fight."

"I don't think that will happen," she assures me. "I know my girl and I know what she wants, whether she's ready to admit it or not. Just give her time, Riley."

DEVYN

IT'S SATURDAY NIGHT and Jackson has taken me to a fancy French restaurant overlooking the Puget Sound. It's a little too stuffy for my tastes, but he likes it and the view is wonderful.

"Welcome to Sur L'Eau," the tuxedoed host says. "Do you have reservations?"

Jackson grabs my hand. "Yes, we do. Williams for two in the private dining room."

The private dining room? I give Jackson a quizzical look but he simply smiles.

The host's face brightens as he grabs two menus. "Of course, monsieur. Please follow me."

We're led to a rectangular room off the main dining area with floor to ceiling windows taking up an entire wall. There are at least a dozen small tables topped with crisp white linens but we're the only people in the room.

The host pulls out my chair. "Madame."

I take a seat. "Thank you."

He hands us our menus and nods to Jackson. "I'll be right back with the champagne you requested with your reservation, monsieur."

"Merci," Jackson says in a perfect French accent.

I wait until we're alone. "Jackson, what's going on?"

He gives me a sheepish smile. "I can't take you out for a nice evening?"

I gesture to our surroundings. "Sure you can...but this is over the top. What's the occasion?"

He waits to respond as our host returns with a corked bottle of champagne and two flutes. He fills each glass and sets the bottle in a bucket of ice next to our table.

"Would you like to hear our specials?"

Jackson shakes his head. "No, thank you."

The waiter gives a short nod. "Very well. Olivia will be your *serveuse* this evening. She should be with you in a few moments."

When our host exits the room I lean over the table. "Jackson, seriously. What's going on? Why all the fanfare?"

He grabs my hand and begins stroking his thumb over my knuckles. "You've been working so hard lately and we've barely seen each other. I thought this would be nice."

I sink into my chair with a knot in my stomach. "This is too much."

He holds up his glass of champagne. "Just relax, Devyn. Should we toast?"

I grab my flute. "What should we toast to?"

He clinks his glass to mine. "To the future."

I take a lengthy sip of bubbly without echoing the sentiment. Thankfully, Jackson doesn't seem to notice. We eat dinner with polite small talk and share a dessert afterwards. The food was great and the atmosphere is lovely but I can't escape this feeling of dread.

Jackson stands and offers his hand. "Dance with me."

I look around the room. "There's no dance floor."

He helps me stand. "We don't need one."

He pulls me into him and we begin swaying to the instrumental music that is piped through the restaurant. He starts trailing kisses down my neck. Public displays of affection are very out of character for him.

"Jackson, what's gotten into you tonight?"

He moves up my neck to nip my ear lobe. "You look so beautiful tonight I can't help myself." He pulls back and looks at me thoughtfully. "We haven't made love in six weeks, Devyn. It's been too long since we've been able to connect. I want to come home with you tonight."

"Oh. Uh…I'm sorry; I've just been so busy at work."

He trails his finger down my cheek. "Don't be sorry. I've been thinking about how to fix this problem we have. I know we talked about you moving in with me several times now but I think I finally understand your hesitation."

"You do?"

He nods. "I do. I understand Nathan is your top priority. You're an incredible mother…it's one of the many things I love about you. And I understand why you wouldn't want to rock the boat with him involved. A child needs stability. You don't want to shack up with your boyfriend because there's always that measure of uncertainty about the future."

He does finally get it. "I couldn't have said it any better myself."

He smiles. "That's why I came up with the perfect solution."

"You did? What's that?"

He pulls back and digs into his pocket. Before I can ask what he's looking for, he drops to one knee. *Please don't.*

He takes my hand and holds out a beautiful diamond and sapphire ring. "Jackson—"

"Shh," he says. "Please let me get this out before I muck it all up. Devyn, I don't want to be your boyfriend anymore. I want to be your husband. I want to be Nathan's stepfather. I want the three of us to live together and be a family. We're good together. It makes sense to take this next step. What do you say? Will you marry me?"

I slam my hand over my mouth to choke back a sob. Jackson's expression tells me he's reading my reaction wrong. He thinks these are happy tears. "I…" How am I going to say this? It's going to crush him. "Jackson…I can't marry you. I'm sorry; but I can't. I'm not ready."

He frowns. "I don't understand. Don't you love me?"

I wipe a tear away. "I do…but it's complicated."

He stands up and brushes himself off. "What's so complicated about it?"

"I…" I can't think of anything to say.

"Is this because of Riley?" he asks. "Is he the reason you won't say yes?"

I can't look him in the eyes. "Jackson, you're such a good man. But I'm just not ready."

He tilts my chin up, forcing me to look at him. "I notice you're not denying it. What's going on, Devyn? Do you still have feelings for him?"

"I…I don't know." I shrug. "Maybe."

Jackson tucks the ring back in his pocket. "I see. Well, that certainly does complicate things."

"Do you hate me?"

He shakes his head and kisses my forehead. "No. Of course not. You need time to digest everything; that's all. I know we're right for each other, Devyn. And I'm confident you'll see that too. Maybe I just need to do a better job convincing you."

I sniff. "Jackson, you're too good to me."

"Nonsense," he says. "I love you. And you love me. Let's just focus on that." He leans over the table to sign the credit card receipt then grabs my purse, handing it to me. "If you don't mind, I'm going to drop you off at home. I just remembered that I need to get up early to meet my mother for breakfast tomorrow."

"You didn't mention anything about breakfast with your mom."

He shrugs. "It slipped my mind." He offers his arm. "Come on, let's get you home."

"Okay," I say.

THIRTY

DEVYN

"HI, DEAR. I'M AFRAID I have some bad news," Rose, Nathan's sitter, says in a hoarse voice.

"What's wrong?" I hold the phone up with my shoulder as I'm pulling Nate's shirt over his head.

"I won't be able to sit with your boy today. I'm afraid I've come down with food poisoning."

"Really?" Ugh! My big pitch is today. This couldn't happen on a worse day. I clear my throat. "I'm so sorry to hear that, Rose. Thanks for letting me know."

She coughs. "I'm sorry, dear."

"Feel better," I say. "Let me know if you need anything."

"Thanks, Devyn. You're a sweet girl."

I end the call and glance at the time. I only have an hour before I have to leave and no clue what to do. Nate's preschool isn't in session on Tuesdays, Drew can't just walk away from his shift, and Rainey is in some training thing for work. I suppose I could call Jackson.

"Crap!" I say.

"What's wrong, Momma?"

I brush Nathan's hair down. "Rose is sick, honey. She's not going to be able to watch you today."

Nathan pumps his little fist in the air. "Yes! That means you get to stay home and play with me today!"

A knot of guilt settles in my stomach from his excitement. "No, baby, I can't. I have a really important meeting at work today. I'm going to call Jackson and see if he can come over."

"Moooooommm," Nathan whines. "I don't wanna play with Jackson all day. He doesn't like my Legos or my dinosaurs! He's boooor-ing!"

Jackson is really kind to Nathan but he's definitely not into playtime. "I'm sorry, buddy, but I don't really have a choice."

"What about Riley?" he asks.

"What about him?"

"He can come over and play with me!" Nathan says excitedly.

I bite my lip. "Oh, I don't know. Riley's probably really busy with work."

He tugs on my suit jacket. "Pweaaase, Momma! Just call him!"

I think about it for a moment. I guess it wouldn't hurt to ask. I kiss Nathan on the forehead. "Go brush your teeth and I'll give him a call."

"Sweet!" he says.

I laugh as I walk down the hall. I scroll through my contacts until I reach Riley's number, hit the call button, and take a deep breath.

He answers after two rings. "Good morning. I wasn't expecting to hear from you until tonight."

"Hi," I say. "I have a huge favor to ask."

I hear him moving around. "Anything. What's up?"

"Rose, Nate's sitter, has food poisoning so she can't watch him. He only has preschool on Monday, Wednesday, and Friday. Drew is on shift at the firehouse until Thursday and Rainey has an annual training thing at work. I'd hate to ask so last minute, but would you by chance be able to take the day off? As you know, my pitch is today. I can't miss it. If it's too much for you, I can call—"

"I'll do it," he interrupts.

"Really? You don't mind babysitting a crazy four-year-old all day?"

"Devyn, he's my son. It's not called babysitting when it's your own kid. I'd be happy to stay with him. It will be nice to finally have one on one time with him."

I smile. "Are you sure it's not too much?"

"I'm positive. I'm looking forward to it. When do you need me?"

I look at the clock. "I need to leave by eight at the latest. Do you think you can make it in time?"

"I can be there by quarter till."

"That's perfect, Rye. Thank you so much. You're really saving my butt here."

"Devyn, I mean it. It's my pleasure. I just got out of the shower so I can leave as soon as I throw some clothes on."

"You're naked right now?" I squeak.

I swear I can see his smile through the phone. "Well, technically I'm wearing a towel but I can lose it if you need me to improve the visual."

I gulp. "Nope. The towel's good."

He laughs. "I'll see you soon, Dev."

"See you soon," I echo.

RILEY

. . .

"OKAY, ALL THE IMPORTANT phone numbers are on the fridge. Pediatrician, Poison Control, my office, etcetera." Devyn's been rattling off instructions for the past ten minutes. "Plus you can always call my cell if there's an emergency."

I smirk. "We'll be fine, Dev."

She offers me a small smile. "Thank you again, Riley."

"Again, it's my pleasure. Now go kick ass with your presentation." I give her a little scoot towards the door.

She looks over her shoulder. "Okay, his booster seat is in the office if you need it, and——"

"I got it the first two times," I say. "Now go. Don't worry about us."

She pauses at the threshold. "I'll try to be home by five. I'll text you if I'm running late."

I can't help myself. I pull her into me and kiss the little crinkle between her brows. "Go. To. Work. And good luck."

She pulls back and blinks a few times. "Uh...okay. Thanks."

I shake my head and close the door behind her. I turn around to find Nathan bouncing on the balls of his feet.

"Hey, buddy," I say. "Are you ready to have a fun day?"

He gestures to the toys in his hands. "You wanna play Transformers?"

I nod. "Sure. But only if I get to be Optimus Prime."

He frowns. "SUCK MY BALLS! I get to be Optimus Pwime!"

I hold my hands up and laugh. "Okay, okay. No need to get so testy." Yep, I went there. "I'll be Bumble Bee."

After Transformers, we moved on to G.I. Joe and now we're building with Legos. I almost forgot how fun playing with the stuff is.

"Hey, Riley?"

"Yeah, dude?"

"Are you my daddy?"

I raise my eyebrows, impressed by his intuitiveness. "Why would you think that?"

He shrugs. "I don't know. Aunt Wainey was telling Momma that I look just like you."

Shit, how am I supposed to answer this? I don't want to lie to the kid but I don't think Devyn would be happy with me if I told him without her. "How would you feel if I was your daddy?"

He scrunches his nose in concentration. "I think you'd be a good daddy."

"Oh yeah?" I ask. "Why's that?"

He shrugs. "You're funner than Jackson. I think he has a stick up his ath-hole."

I bark in laughter before composing myself. "That's not nice, buddy. And don't say asshole."

"Put a dollar in the jar!"

"What?" I ask. "I was just repeating what you said!"

"Doesn't matter. Momma says you have to put a dollar in the jar when you say a bad word."

I stand up and offer my hand. "Come on, bud. Why don't you show me where the jar is and then I'll make you some lunch."

"I want peanut butter jelly!"

I smile. "My favorite."

Thankfully, Nate dropped the subject during lunch. Later in the day we're sitting on the couch to watch some cartoons. He lets out a big yawn about twenty minutes in and snuggles into me. "Hey, Riley?"

"Yeah, bud?"

"It's okay if you wanna be my daddy but you have to

wuv my mommy because mommies and daddies are 'posta be in wuv. Do you wuv my mommy?"

I wrap my arm around him. "Yeah, big guy; I do."

Nate falls asleep in my arms and I just sit there watching him for who knows how long. He's so fucking perfect I want to cry like a girl. He looks really uncomfortable so I scoop him up and bring him into his bedroom. I don't know if he should be napping this late in the day but I can't bring myself to wake him. The little guy wore me out; I can't imagine how tired he must be. I hear the door opening right as I'm leaving his room. I look down at my watch and see that Devyn's a half hour early. I walk down the hall to greet her and pause when I enter the living room.

Jackson sets his keys on the side table. "Hey," he says. "Where's the kid?"

I nod my head towards the hallway. "He fell asleep. I put him down for a nap."

We stand there in some sort of silent showdown. Neither one of us seems willing to talk to the other. Fuck, this is awkward.

I decide to be the bigger man. "Devyn's not home. But I'm guessing you knew that already."

He smirks. "I did. But she'll be home soon. I was hoping to talk to you before she gets here."

I stare at his keys. "You have a key to her place, huh?"

"Of course," he says dismissively.

"What'd you want to talk about?" I snap.

He walks across the room and takes a seat at the small dining table. "I wanted to clear the air—man to man."

I cross my arms over my chest. "Clear the air about *what* exactly?"

He sits back and crosses his ankle over his knee. "Look... I know you're going to stick around so I figured we should get this out of the way. I know the real story between you and Devyn. I feel bad that you've missed out on being a dad when you clearly want to be involved. What she did may not have been right, but she wasn't exactly thinking clearly at the time."

I lean against the wall. "Devyn doesn't need you to defend her. I'm not mad about it. We both made shitty decisions. What's important is that I'm here now and I plan to stay."

"Right," he nods. "Well, I just thought you should know that the guilt has been plaguing her for years. She thought about finding you several times but she was afraid you'd reject the kid. He means everything to her and she was terrified that you wouldn't react how she wanted you to."

"It's a moot point now," I say. "I love Nathan. And she knows that. She also knows that I'm going to be the best damn father I can possibly be."

"I understand," he says. "That's why I wanted to make sure there wasn't any animosity between us. Let's face it; this could be very awkward."

"*Could* be?" I scoff.

Jackson is oblivious to my sarcasm. "Anyway, I wanted to thank you."

"Thank me for what?"

"For the way things panned out," he replies. "Don't get me wrong; I'm not saying I wanted Devyn to go through the heartbreak, but everything that she endured has led her to me. She and Nathan are in my world because you screwed up once upon a time. I helped her move on and we forged a strong bond because of it. I know you're going to be around since the whole paternity thing is bound to surface sooner or later, so we need to figure out a way to co-exist peacefully. For Devyn's and Nathan's sakes."

"How mature of you," I mutter.

He assesses me with a cold glare. "I guess being polite

isn't going to get my point across so I'll just come out and say it."

I gesture for him to continue. "By all means."

He smirks again. "Look, I can tell that you have...*feelings* for Devyn. But the fact is, she and I will be married soon. Which means that I will officially be Nathan's stepfather. *I'll* be the one warming Devyn's bed at night and the one who will hopefully give Nate a little brother or sister."

I bite my tongue and clench my fists. "Married, huh? What makes you think that?"

He shrugs. "I proposed the other night. She didn't tell you?"

"No, she failed to mention it," I say through gritted teeth.

"Huh," he says. "She must want to break it to you lightly. I guess I beat her to it."

I nod towards the front door. "Yeah, well, I'll be sure to bring it up when she comes home. I'll let her know you stopped by."

He chuckles. "I'm not going anywhere, Riley. Devyn asked me to come relieve you from kid duty. She'll be home soon and we'd like some *alone time* if you catch my drift."

"Well, as nice as it was of you to offer your *services*, I'm fine staying here until she gets home. Besides, I think Devyn would've called if she wanted me to leave."

He eyes my cell phone that's sitting on the breakfast bar. "Have you checked your phone lately? She said she was going to text you."

I frown as I walk over to my phone. I pull up the messages and sure enough, there's one from her.

Devyn: Hey, I'm running behind. The presentation went great. I can't wait to tell you about it! Jackson should be there soon to take over for you. Thanks again for saving me.

"Well? Is there a message from her?" Jackson asks.

I shove my phone in my back pocket and grab my keys off the counter. "Yep."

He stands and walks over to the door, opening it for me. "Thanks for babysitting. I'll take it from here."

I step into the hallway. "Tell Nathan I said goodbye when he wakes up."

Jackson gives me a smug grin. "Will do. Have a good night, Riley. I know Devyn and I will."

He shuts the door. It's a good thing too because I was just about to punch that superior expression off his face. I can't believe that asshole! He clearly thinks he's won but he has no idea who he's fucking with. I'm not giving up without one helluva fight. If he wants to play dirty, game on.

THIRTY-ONE

RILEY

BRODY INVITED ME TO Kelly's Bar & Grill for drinks on Friday night. This place is my favorite kind of bar. They host a dozen screens broadcasting sports, a couple pool tables, darts, decent food, and a fine selection of beer. Our little group usually meets here because the atmosphere is great and the employees are cool. Normally, it's the perfect place to unwind after a long work week. Tonight is the exception to that.

I hold my arm out to halt Brody. "What the fuck is he doing here?"

Brody follows my gaze and sees Drew, Rainey, Devyn, and *Jackson* sitting at a table. Jackson's chair is right next to Devyn's and his fucking hand is all over her thigh.

Brody shrugs. "I don't know, man. He's never joined us before. Like *ever*. I've really only seen him in passing before now."

I know *exactly* what he's doing here. He must've known

that I was joining them and he felt the need to remind me who Devyn belongs to. We'll see about that.

"Asshole," I mutter.

We continue walking towards the table when Brody whispers, "Don't make a scene, dude."

I take the empty chair directly across from Devyn. "Hey, Dev."

I've been on edge ever since I left her house on Tuesday. I stayed up for hours that night waiting for her usual pre-bedtime call. It never came and she texted me the next day saying she crashed early. I couldn't stop thinking about the fact that she and Jackson were together and my imagination went into overdrive. I've been blowing her off ever since, saying I've been working late. I needed time to cool off.

She blushes. "Oh. Hey, Rye. I didn't think you'd be joining us tonight."

I smirk. "Why's that?"

She starts wringing her hands together. "I just thought you might be working late again."

"Nope." I say the word with a pop at the end.

"Hi there. Can I get you guys a drink?" the waitress asks. I look over and see a cute little brunette who's leaning over to give me a perfect view of her ample cleavage. I catch Devyn watching us out of the corner of my eye.

I look at her nametag and give her my infamous panty-melting grin. "Hi, Brigitte. My buddy and I here would love some beers. How about you surprise us?" I wink for added effect.

Brigitte smiles. "Sure. I think I can do that. I'll be right back."

Brody gives me a *what the fuck* look and Devyn glares at Brigitte's retreating back. I know this is risky but I can't seem to help myself at the moment. I'm hoping to spark the same green-eyed monster in Devyn that is raging inside of me right now. When she looks my way, I can see that it's working.

Drew slugs Brody's shoulder. "Hey, asshole. You want to go shoot some pool?"

"Uh…sure. Riley you want to join us?"

My eyes never leave Devyn. "No, thanks, man. I'm good right where I'm at."

Brody and Drew get up from the table, laughing at something as they walk away.

Rainey takes a sip of beer and clears her throat. "So, Dev, you were just about to tell us about your big pitch. How'd it go?"

Devyn's face lights up. "It was perfect. *I was perfect*. I really think I nailed this account!"

Rainey smiles. "Way to go, girl! When do you find out?"

Jackson pulls Devyn into him and kisses the corner of her mouth. "She should know on Monday. I know she's going to get it though. She's worked so hard on this client; more than any before. They'd be fools to turn her down."

Devyn smiles shyly at his praise. "Thank you, Jackson."

He pushes her hair behind her ear and nibbles her lobe. "Anytime, babe. I'm proud of you."

I ball my hands into fists under the table and clench my jaw. I have to remind myself that jumping across the table to pummel this guy isn't going to accomplish anything. "That's great, Dev. You always have been the best at everything you do." I lean over and lower my voice slightly. "And I do mean *everything*."

She shifts uncomfortably and blushes. "Thanks, Rye."

Rainey jumps out of her chair and grabs my elbow. "Wow, I need another beer. Riley, why don't you come with me so I don't have to ruin my streak of not paying for my own drinks?"

205

I look down at her half full glass. "Is there something wrong with that one?"

She grabs the glass and chugs it in two long gulps. "I'm reaaaallly thirsty. I can't wait for the waitress to come back here." She grabs Devyn's wine glass and finishes that off as well. "See? Now Devyn needs a new drink too. Come on."

She pulls my arm, leading me towards the bar. When we get there I say, "Now do you want to tell me what that was really about?"

She thunks me on the forehead. "Idiot!"

"Ow!" I shout as I rub my forehead. "What the hell was that for?"

"Could you *be* more obvious?"

The bartender takes our order as I glare at her. Then I say, "What the fuck are you talking about?"

"Oh, puh-leez," she says. "You and Jackson are practically measuring dicks out there! You're making Devyn really uncomfortable."

I frown. "I'm not trying to make her uncomfortable."

"Really?" she sneers. "'Surprise me with a beer, Brigitte.' What the fuck was that? Are you trying to get the waitress into bed?"

"No!"

"Well, then what were you doing? Because I'm pretty sure her phone number will be with your drink when we get back." She gestures to our table where Brigitte is delivering two beers and setting a folded napkin to the side of my glass.

I rake my hand through my hair. "Fuck. I don't know. I was trying to make Devyn jealous to get her out of her controlled little shell. I would never consider going out with the waitress."

She rolls her eyes. "You're playing this all wrong, Riley. Making Devyn jealous isn't the answer."

I throw my hands up. "Well, then what is? Please tell me you know because I have no fucking clue!"

"I told you she needs to come to terms with this on her own. Don't push her because you can't be patient." She grabs my elbow and prompts me to start walking. "Let's get back before they get suspicious."

We return to our table and I decide to take Rainey's advice. I unfold the napkin out of curiosity and find Brigitte's phone number. I tuck it into my shirt pocket so Devyn doesn't see it, planning to throw it away later. I go through two beers before Drew and Brody return to the table. I shift my attention to them as much as possible so I don't obsess over the way Jackson can't seem to keep his hands off Devyn. He's touching her and kissing her at every possible opportunity. All I see is red by the time I've finished my third beer. I mean seriously, is the PDA really necessary? He's practically humping her at the table, for fuck's sake! And she definitely doesn't seem into it. I can see her growing more and more irritated as he continues. Doesn't he realize that she's inching her chair away from his?

Devyn stands. "I need to go to the bathroom." She quickly walks away without another word.

I count to twenty and pretend to read something on my phone. "I'll be right back. I have to check in with work."

I duck away and head in the direction that Devyn fled. I spot the women's restroom and wait right outside the door.

Devyn jumps when she sees me upon exiting. "Riley! What are you—"

I cut her off when I shove her into the bathroom and shut the door. I turn the lock and check under the stalls for feet. We're alone. Good.

"Why are you even with that tool?" I growl. "You two don't have anything in common."

Her cheeks redden. "What the hell kind of question is

that? He's a good man. He's been nothing but kind to me and Nathan over the years."

"Kind?" I sneer. "Wow, that's not the word I'd want my woman to use when describing me."

"What's wrong with kind?"

"Kind is boring. Kind is safe. Kind is NOT passion. Fireworks. Kind does not get you off. Kind is the word I'd use to describe my accountant." Her eyes widen with that last word. "Oh my God, he's an *accountant*?"

"What's wrong with that?" she asks. "It's a perfectly respectable way to make a living."

"Jesus Christ, Devyn. What happened to not settling? That's exactly what you're doing! There's no way Mr. Stick-Up-His-Ass back there knows how to work your body over until you can't see straight. Has he ever even made you come?"

She blushes and screams, "Not everything is about sex, Riley!"

"No, it's not," I admit. "But you can't spend the rest of your life with someone who doesn't know how to satisfy you."

"I never said that he didn't!"

"You didn't have to!" I scream back.

She throws her hands up in the air. "What do you suggest? Who should I be with?" She laughs mockingly, pissing me off. She reaches into my shirt pocket and pulls out the napkin. "What's this, Riley?"

I try to grab it as she unfolds it. "Nothing. I was going to toss it."

She laughs again as she reads it. "Right. Why should I believe you?"

"Because it's the truth!" I shout.

She waves the napkin in the air. "And I'm supposed to just take your word for it? You don't want a real relationship,

Riley! This phone number proves that. You can't do long term monogamy!"

I grab it from her and throw it on the floor. "I didn't want the fucking number! I don't want *anyone* else's fucking number!"

"Then what do you want, Rye? *What the hell* do you want?"

"YOU! All I've ever wanted since the day we met was you!"

She's stunned. "What?"

I decide actions speak louder than words. Fuck Rainey's advice. Devyn needs a reminder of how explosive we are together. I advance upon her and cage her against the wall.

"What are you—" she starts to ask.

I answer her with my lips pressed against hers. She fights me for half a second before she moans, pulling me into her. It's just as good between us as I remember. Better even. We're saying everything we need to with our lips and our tongues. She kisses me back with so much fucking passion it's like it's been bottled up all these years. She runs her fingers through my hair, yanking forcefully as she demands more. Never breaking the kiss, I grab her legs and wrap them around my hips. I grind into her and she tightens her legs around me to press into me deeper. My dick is harder than steel, dying to be inside this woman where it belongs.

I break away from her mouth and move down her neck. "God, I hate that I can smell his cologne on you."

Devyn tenses and pulls back to disentangle herself. I step back and meet her eyes. Shit, she looks like she's about to cry.

She points toward the bathroom door. "Go, Riley! I'm not this girl. You can't just go around saying things like that, kissing anyone you please."

"I wasn't the only one doing the kissing," I remind her.

She groans in frustration. "Just go! I'll be out in a minute."

I try to get a read on her but she's shutting down. "Dev—"

A tear drops down her face. "GO, RILEY!"

I step back and take a deep breath. I slam my hand against the door. "Fuck!" I unlock it and pull it open with much more force than necessary. Before walking away, I lower my voice and say, "I'll give you time to get your shit together, but don't walk away from this, Devyn. Don't walk away from *us*."

DEVYN

I TURN TOWARD THE mirror and stare at my reflection after Riley stormed away. God, what am I doing? My hair is tousled and my lip gloss has been sucked off entirely. I make myself as presentable as possible and take a deep breath. I can do this. I'll just go out there, tell everyone I have a headache, and then Jackson and I can leave so we can talk privately. I can't put this off any longer. My reaction towards Riley just now proved that. It's not fair to Jackson to continue along the path we're on.

I make my way back to the table a moment later. Riley is noticeably absent and the remaining four are suspiciously quiet.

Drew clears his throat. "Uh…Riley had to go—said he had something to take care of."

"Oh." I look up at Jackson. His ears are cherry red and his eyes are narrowed into slits.

Rainey touches me lightly on the shoulder. "Everything okay, hon?"

I fidget nervously as all eyes are on me. "Um...I have a headache. I think I need to call it a night."

Jackson stands without a word and begins walking towards the door.

I nod towards him. "Um...I guess we're going now. Lorraine, I'll call you later."

"You'd better," she says.

Jackson barely says a word to me on the entire drive home. The tension in the air is suffocating. I don't think I've ever seen him angry before but that's definitely what this is. Does he sense that something happened between me and Riley?

He pulls against the curb in front of my building.

"You're not coming in?" I ask.

He shakes his head. "No. I don't think that would be wise right now."

I shift my body towards him. "Jackson, I really think we need to have a talk."

"So talk."

"Here? Can't you just come up for a little while?"

He sighs. "Devyn, if you have something to say to me, please just say it already."

I take a deep breath. "I kissed Riley."

"Did he kiss you, or did you kiss him?"

"Does it matter?"

"Yes, I think it does."

I bite my lip. "He kissed me...but then I kissed him back."

"I see," Jackson says, perfectly composed.

"C'mon, Jackson, how can you be so calm about this? I just told you I kissed another man! It's okay to be angry."

"Oh, I'm angry," he says. "But I think there's already been enough shouting this evening."

"What? What does that mean?"

His face flushes. "You were in a fucking bathroom, Devyn. Fifty feet from our table. Ever hear of something called bathroom acoustics? I heard *everything*. The entire group heard everything. Well, except when at one point the conversation ended entirely. I suppose that's when the kissing commenced."

I blanch. "Oh my God. Jackson, I'm sooo, sooo sorry. I never planned for anything like this to happen."

He releases a cynical laugh. "What the hell were you thinking, Devyn? Do I make you that unhappy?"

"What? No, of course not!" I try grabbing his hand but he pulls away. "Jackson, I am truly sorry. You're a good man. You've been so wonderful to me and Nathan."

"Just not good enough," he mutters.

"Jackson, this has nothing to do with you."

He rolls his eyes. "Really, Dev? It's not you; it's me. That's your excuse?"

I take a deep breath and blink back my tears. "You deserve someone who didn't give their heart away years ago. When we got together, I really thought I was ready to move on. And things between us have been good. But I've always held back. I *know* you know that, Jackson. I just don't think either one of us was willing to admit why."

He sighs. "So you're going to be with Riley?"

"I don't know," I say, "but continuing this relationship isn't fair to either one of us. Riley's reappearance brought feelings to the surface that I thought I buried a long time ago. I need to figure out what I'm going to do about them."

"So we're breaking up?"

I nod as a single tear falls. "We're breaking up."

RILEY

. . .

I DRIVE AROUND FUMING until I end up at the house I just bought. I park against the curb and just stare at everything this house represents. It's everything I've dreamed of but none of that matters if Devyn isn't in the picture. Well, that's not totally true, because I *will* be a constant presence in my son's life no matter what, but we can't be the family unit that I'm picturing if she's married to that asshole! How could she accept his proposal? Wait a second…was she wearing a ring? Could he have lied? Fuck! I can't remember! I saw nothing but red as he continuously touched her every chance he got.

I take a few deep breaths to calm down. Only one way to know for sure. I pick up my phone and dial her number.

She answers right before my call goes to voicemail. She doesn't say anything but I can hear her breathing.

"Dev, are you there?"

She blows out a breath. "Yeah, I'm here."

"What's wrong?"

"Do you really need to ask that, Rye? My head is messed up. This probably isn't the best time to talk. I need to sort through some things."

Is she crying? "Devyn, talk to me."

She sighs. "Jackson and I broke up."

Did I seriously just hear that? "So you're not going to marry him?"

"What? Who said that I was *ever* going to marry him?"

"He did," I reply. "Well, not exactly. But he told me that he proposed and then implied that you said yes."

She groans. "I'm such a horrible person."

"Why would you say that? He's the asshole who lied!"

"Don't call him names, Rye. I'm the one who lied to him for two-and-a-half years. It's bad enough that I've been lying to myself. He didn't need to be dragged into it. He's a good man. He's just not the right man."

My ears perk up. "And who is?"

She ignores my question. "I need you to do me a favor."

"Name it."

"I need you to call your realtor. I want to show Nathan his new bedroom this weekend."

I'm smiling so wide my cheeks hurt. "Does that mean what I think it means? Are you agreeing to move in with me?"

"Yeah, Riley...I am. Balls to the wall, baby."

THIRTY-TWO

DEVYN

"HERE IT IS," RILEY says.

We just pulled in the driveway of Riley's new home. *Our* new home, rather. God, that's so strange to say but at the same time, it feels so right. The house is a Craftsman style, painted light blue with white trim. I smile when I see the white wooden swing hanging by some chains. I can easily picture relaxing on it under the covered porch, lying on Riley's lap, with a cold beer in hand. The yard is meticulously landscaped and has a few mature trees offering shade.

"It's perfect," I say.

Riley smiles as he exits the vehicle. "Wait until you see the inside."

I get out of the car and open the back door to help Nathan out. He immediately runs up the stairs and tries the front door.

Riley laughs. "Whoa, slow down there, buddy. I need to enter the code to get the key."

LAURA LEE

Nathan scrunches his brow. "How come we hafta have a secret code?"

Riley looks at his phone and punches in the combo his realtor gave him to unlock the key box. "This funny looking thing is just temporary. It will be gone once the sale of the house is final."

Nate bounces on the balls of his feet as he waits for Riley to open the door. As soon as the lock unlatches, Nathan sprints inside.

"Nathan! Wait for us!" I say.

Riley takes my hand and leads me inside. He grabs the back of Nathan's shirt as he runs by. "Hold up, dude."

Nathan stops mid-stride. "Aw, man!"

Riley chuckles. "I thought the three of us could look at the house together. Does that sound okay with you, buddy?"

Nate rolls his eyes. "If we hafta."

I grab his hand. "Yes, we have to. Now behave yourself, mister."

"Aw, mom," Nathan whines.

Riley smiles. "So, what do you think?"

The main level consists primarily of one big open space with dark plank wooden flooring throughout. The living room takes up the front portion and boasts a gas fireplace with large windows that allow tons of natural light to filter in. A gorgeous kitchen with an oversized island is towards the back. The cabinets are white, the countertops are quartz, and the appliances are stainless. There's a nice-sized space in between that could easily accommodate a six-person table.

"It's ginormeous, mommy!" Nathan exclaims.

"It sure is, baby. Riley, this is incredible. It looks like something off HGTV."

Riley chuckles as he moves about opening doors for me to peek inside. "Coat closet, powder room, and pantry. The bedrooms and laundry are upstairs."

Riley tugs on Nate's hand. "Do you want to go see your bedroom?"

"I get my own bedroom?" Nate asks.

Riley nods. "You sure do."

Nathan scrunches his face and looks up towards me. "But where will you be, Mommy?"

I make eye contact with Riley as I reply. "I'll be right here with you, baby. The three of us are going to live here together."

"What about Unca' Drew?"

I kneel in front of him. "Uncle Drew is going to stay right where he is. I'm sure he'll come over for lots of visits though. And if you miss him, I can take you to see him too."

"Promise?"

Riley ruffles his hair. "We promise. You wanna go pick out your new room?"

Nathan's face lights up. "I can pick?"

Riley nods. "You sure can. Mommy gets the biggest bedroom but you can choose your room from the other two."

"Then you get the one I don't want?" Nate asks.

Riley gulps and looks at me. "That's up to your mommy, dude. She gets to choose where I sleep."

I feel the blush creeping into my cheeks as his words sink in. He's going to let me set the pace. Even though I've agreed to move in, he's not going to pressure me into a relationship with him. We haven't really had a chance to talk about it yet, but I meant what I said earlier. I'm pushing full throttle here; I've waited long enough for this opportunity. The three of us can finally be together every day. Riley and I can be together as a couple and we can raise our child together. I can't think of anything that I want more.

Nathan giggles. "So she can make you sleep in the toilet?"

Riley laughs. "Yep. She sure can." He holds out his hand. "Let's go pick out your room, buddy."

Nathan grabs on and Riley extends his free hand towards me. I clasp our fingers together and follow as he leads us up the stairs. There are two rooms for him to choose from, each one about ten by ten in size with a full bath in between.

Nate points to the one on the right. "I want that one!" He runs into the room and starts pretending to be an airplane.

Riley stands in the doorway watching him. "Hey, dude, are you going to be okay in here for a few minutes? I want to show Mommy her room."

In reply, Nathan continues spreading his arms and making plane noises.

Riley turns to me. "You ready?"

I nod. "Lead the way."

RILEY

I TAKE HER INTO the master bedroom. She trails her fingers over the light gray walls and walks across the room to perch herself on the window seat. She tilts her face towards the sun and looks out the window.

She presses her hand on the glass. "Oh, wow! You can see the water from up here."

I smile. "You like it?"

"I love it, Rye. It's absolutely perfect."

I offer my hand to help her stand. "Let me show you the master bath."

She takes my hand and allows me to lead her into the attached bathroom. She looks around the room from the marble double vanity to the rainhead shower and finally to the deep soaker tub.

She raises her eyebrows suggestively. "A tub built for two. Brings back some good memories."

"Huh. Look at that. I didn't even notice."

She laughs and smacks me playfully. "Right."

She peeks into the small walk-in closet and steps back into the bedroom.

I shove my hands in my pockets. "So…"

She tucks a hair behind her ear. "So…"

We share a heated glance but don't say a word. I can't stand not touching her anymore so I stalk towards her until she backs into the wall. She gasps when I place my hands on her hips and lean over to whisper in her ear.

"You're not really going to make me sleep in the toilet, are you?"

She chuckles as she wraps her arms around my waist. "Hmm, I haven't decided yet."

I place soft kisses down the nape of her neck. "No? Maybe I can help you decide."

She moans when I pull her against me. "How are you going to do that?"

"I have some ideas…"

She ghosts her hand over my denim-clad erection. "Such as?"

I groan as I press into her palm. "Honey, you keep doing that and I'm about to show you every idea I've ever had up against this wall."

She shivers. "That sounds promising."

I pull back to look her in the eyes. "You think so?"

She bites her lower lip. "Very much so."

I smile as I hover over that sexy mouth of hers. I pause for a second, giving her a chance to back out before I press my lips against hers. She responds instantly, opening so I can slide my tongue between her lips. Fuck, she's so warm and tastes so sweet.

I deepen the kiss, thrusting my tongue inside her mouth as I grind my body against hers. She pulls me into her, practically climbing me like a tree trunk. She keeps making these sexy little whimpers like she's so hungry for me, she can't get enough. Desperate to feel her bare skin, I glide my fingertips beneath her shirt and brush the underside of her breast.

She gasps. "Oh, Rye."

"Whatcha doin'?" Nathan asks.

Shit! We both break apart instantly. I didn't even hear him come into the room. Devyn smoothes her shirt down. She looks down and sees the tent in my pants and smirks. She steps in front of me so I can hide behind her as we face our son.

"Hey, buddy," she says.

"Why were you making those funny sounds, Momma?"

Her eyes widen. "Um, your daddy and I were um...we uh...we were just making silly animal noises."

Holy shit! Does she realize what she just said? Did Nathan catch it?

I know the moment it hits her. Her jaw drops and she gives me a look that says, *Oh my God, did I really just do that?*

I adjust myself and hunch down to the floor. "Hey, bud. Remember when you asked me if I was your daddy?"

Devyn's eyes widen. Oops, I guess I forgot to tell her about that.

Nathan nods. "Yep."

"And do you remember what you said to me?"

"That it's okay if you wanna be my daddy but you have to wuv my mommy."

I smile. "That's right, big guy. And do you remember what I said to you after that?"

He bounces on his feet. "Uh huh. You wuv her."

I glance up at Devyn and she has tears pooling in her eyes as she silently watches our exchange. "That's right. I did. So are you okay if I'm your daddy?"

Nate scrunches his little face while contemplating my question. "Can I punch you in the nuts?"

I bark in laughter. "What? No, dude. You can't punch me in the nuts. You probably shouldn't do that to anyone."

"Are you gonna get mad at me like Momma does when I say a bad word?"

I smile. "Probably. So what do you say? Can I be your dad?"

He shrugs. "I guess. As long as you don't act like a duthbag."

"Nathan!" Devyn scolds.

I crack a smile. "I'll do my best, buddy."

THIRTY-THREE

DEVYN

MONDAY MORNINGS ARE HARD enough but the fact that I can't stop thinking about Riley is making it worse than usual. I keep flashing back to our little make-out session at the new house and what happened afterwards. I smile when I think about how the whole daddy reveal went with Nathan. I've been building it up in my mind for so long I never considered he'd be so nonchalant about it. I know it's too early to know for sure, but my gut is telling me that he's going to naturally accept Riley being a part of his life.

There's a light tap on my cubicle wall. "Hey, Devyn. Do you have a few moments?"

I look up and see Gary Styles, the VP of Creative Marketing. "Sure, Mr. Styles."

He smiles. "Now, Devyn how many times do I have to tell you? Please, call me Gary."

I blush. "Sorry, *Gary*."

He nods behind him. "Let's head to the conference room."

I stand up to follow him. "Sure."

We walk down the hallway that bisects the art department from the copy department until we reach the glass-enclosed conference room towards the end. Mr. Styles...er, Gary, pulls out a chair for me at the long, rectangular table.

"Please, have a seat."

I notice that Norah from Human Resources is here as well. What the heck is going on?

"Is everything okay?" I ask.

Gary takes a seat. "Of course. I just wanted a little privacy." He sees me eyeing Norah and adds, "Norah is here to help make things official."

I scrunch my brows. "Make *what* official?"

Gary folds his hands together on the table. "I spoke with the people from Sage Management this morning."

That's the account I've been working so hard on. Did something go wrong? "And? Did they decide to go with someone else?"

He chuckles. "On the contrary. They've agreed to a three-year contract with the possibility of renewal. They were incredibly impressed with your ideas. They said, and I quote, 'You'd be a moron not to do everything in your power to keep that one happy.'"

"They did?"

He nodded. "Indeed. So...that's why I've invited Norah to this meeting. You've been with us for almost three years now and we've been nothing but impressed with your work ethic, creativity, and drive. As you know, Rena Schwartz recently moved over to the media department which leaves us with an opening for Creative Director. We'd like to offer that position to you. Should you accept, you'll take the lead on the Sage account as well as a few other long term clients.

You'd have your own office complete with administrative assistant. You will lead the art and copywriting team you work with now and report to me directly. In addition to this, there's a substantial salary increase. So what do you think? Do you want the job?"

I'm smiling so wide my cheeks hurt. "Of course, sir. I'd be honored."

He stands and shakes my hand. "Great. I need to head into another meeting so I'll leave you here with Norah to work out the details. Congratulations, Devyn. You've earned it."

"Thank you so much. You won't regret it."

"I have no doubt," he says as he walks out of the room.

RILEY

I'M WALKING INTO THE production plant for a meeting when my cell phone rings. I duck into a small alcove and pull it out of my jacket pocket. I smile when I see Devyn's face on the display.

"Hello, beautiful."

"Hi," she says excitedly. "I have news. Do you have a few minutes?"

I look at the time. "I have a meeting in about ten minutes so I can spare a few. What's this news of yours?"

"I got the job!" she squeals. "It's effective on the first of next month. I can give you the details later but there's a huge raise, I get an assistant, an office, the whole nine yards. It's not normal to jump into this position for at least another couple of years but the position opened and they offered it to me anyway!"

"That's great, baby. Congratulations."

"Thank you," she says. "God, Riley. I can't believe how perfectly everything is falling into place. It makes me nervous. It almost seems too good to be true."

"We should celebrate tonight," I suggest.

"I can't," she says. "I'm meeting the guys at Kelly's for Monday Night Football."

"So I'll join you. I should be able to get out of here in time."

"Really?" she asks.

"Sure. Unless…you don't want me to?"

"No, of course I want you there," she insists. "It's just…well, it would be our first official outing *together*. Are you sure you're ready for that?"

"Did you change your mind? About being all in?" I hold my breath waiting for her reply. Fuck, I don't know what I'll do if she says yes.

"No way, Rye. Balls to the friggin' wall, baby."

I let out a relieved sigh. "Well, then it's a date. I'll see you around five."

THIRTY-FOUR

DEVYN

RILEY IS ALREADY AT the table when I walk into the bar. I get a goofy grin on my face when he starts walking towards me with a sexy swagger.

As he reaches me he whispers, "Are we allowed to kiss in front of them?"

I look behind him and see everyone staring at us, not even trying to be discreet. "Sure."

Riley moves in for a chaste kiss which quickly escalates into something much more appropriate in private.

"Damn it, am I going to have to see this all the time now?" Drew complains.

We break apart and laugh as we take a seat.

Brody takes a sip of beer. "So, what's the deal? Are you two officially an item now?"

Riley and I look at each other.

"Yep," Riley replies. "We sure are."

Brody lifts his beer in toast. "Well, all hail the Magic Pussy, brother!"

I narrow my eyes at Riley. "I'm sorry, but 'all hail' the *what*?"

Riley looks embarrassed. "Ignore him. He's an idiot."

Brody gives Riley the finger. "I'd rather be an idiot than pussy whipped."

Riley smiles at me. "If that's what I am, I'm good with that. You'll see what I mean when it happens to you."

"Ha! Never going to happen, dude," Brody says.

I lean in to kiss Riley again. "You're whipped, huh?"

He smiles. "Abso-fucking-lutely. And proud of it, baby."

RILEY

AFTER GETTING DEVYN A beer, I clear my throat. "So, Devyn has some exciting news."

"What's up, Dee?" Rainey asks.

I swear the smile Devyn gets on her face lights up the room. "It turns out I nailed that account I was telling you about. I got the promotion I wanted!"

A round of whoops and congratulations go around.

"There's more," I say. "I bought a house on Mercer Island."

Drew whistles. "Fancy neighborhood for someone living the bachelor life."

I raise an eyebrow at Devyn asking for permission to proceed. With her eyes, she gives me the go ahead. "Yeah... about that. I'm not moving in alone. Nathan and Devyn are coming with me."

"Ah, fuck," Drew whines while everyone else offers their congratulations again.

Drew leans over and mock whispers. "You sure about this, little sis? You just got back together with the guy. I know you have the kid to think about but you two don't even know each other anymore."

She shakes her head. "That's not true, Drew. I know it seems fast—I know we haven't caught up on everything that's happened over the past five years—but we're still the same people together, only it's better now. I know what I'm doing."

Drew raises his beer. "Well, then I guess it's my job to give you my blessing." He gives me a stern look. "But don't forget what I said earlier. You hurt her and I'll hurt *you*."

"No worries there, man," I assure him. "I have no intention of ever doing that again."

Brody claps Drew on the back. "Well, now that the bodily threats are out of the way, let's celebrate! Big brother here would be happy to buy a round of shots to offer his blessing. Right, buddy?"

Drew rolls his eyes and grunts.

Brody laughs and calls our waitress over. "Hey, Jessica. Can we get a round of Patròn for everyone? Put it on the big sulky guy's tab here."

"Sure thing, guys," Jessica laughs.

We drink our shots when they arrive and trade jibes while watching the game. As I look around the table I can't help but think what a lucky sonofabitch I am. I have a great group of friends, the most incredible son anyone could ever ask for, and the most amazing girl by my side. Devyn offers me a shy smile when she catches me staring at her. My God, she's beautiful. I can't imagine ever getting over the excitement that I feel every time I look at her. And it's not just her physical features. She fucking radiates goodness, compassion, love, and this sexiness that she doesn't seem to be aware of, but it's inherently a part of her. She challenges me like no other. She keeps me grounded. She makes me want to be the best version of myself. I know that I'd be an entirely different man without her in my life.

She slyly moves her hand over my thigh, making me alter my thoughts about her inability to recognize her own sexiness.

Her fingers creep up higher and higher until they reach the bulge behind my fly. Her pinky lazily moves up and down over my dick. She gives me a saucy smile when I start rising to the occasion, confirming that she knows exactly what she's doing. She leans into me slightly and her entire hand joins in on the action. Fuck, she's practically giving me a hand job under the table in front of everyone! I'm going to embarrass myself pretty fucking quickly if she keeps this up.

Without warning, Devyn suddenly releases her grip and stands up. "I have to go to the bathroom. Be right back."

I jump up so fast, I have to save my chair from toppling over. "Yeah...me too. What she said."

I practically run after her and catch her in the hallway to the bathroom. I cage her against a door that's marked *Employees Only* and grind my hard-on into her backside. "You're going to pay for that, you little temptress."

She arches her back, pressing herself into me. "Oh yeah? What are you going to do about it?"

I try the knob to the door and it's unlocked. I peek my head into a storage closet. *Perfect!*

I open the door wider and shove her inside. "You'll see."

I pin her against the wall and our lips instantly crash into each other. Her moans are like fuel, igniting this flame of desire that's always present when I'm anywhere near her. She fists my hair and meets every stroke of my tongue with ravenous strokes of her own. My dick feels like it's about to burst through my zipper but my thoughts shift away from relieving the ache to give her more pleasure.

I untuck her blouse, being a little rougher than I probably should but I need to feel her skin. I bunch the material up and I'm rewarded with a pale pink lace bra. Best of all, it closes in the front. As I pop the clasp, I silently thank the genius that invented these things. Her tits spring free and my mouth instantly attacks them. I take one pretty pink tip into my mouth while I mold the other with my hand. She's curvier than she was before, pretty much everywhere, but especially here. I can't wait to get my hands on the rest of her.

" Rye," she pants.

Devyn hooks her leg around mine and her pencil skirt starts riding up her thigh. I grab her with both hands and shove it up further, then I pick her up and wrap her legs around my hips. She shivers when I run my finger over her matching panties. We both watch as I slip my index finger beneath the fabric and trace her silky smooth skin.

I smile when I get to the center of her body and realize that she no longer has that little strip of curls. "This is different."

She gasps when I move my finger downward. "You like it?"

I dip my hand even lower and find her soaking wet. Fuck, I think I'm going to jizz in my pants like a teenager. "I love it, baby. I can't wait to put my mouth all over you."

I push a finger inside and she gasps loudly. "Oh God, yes!"

I pump my fingers in and out. "You're so wet, baby. I think you liked getting me all worked up under the table. Didn't you?" I nibble her neck while I continue to work her down below. I stop moving when she doesn't answer.

"What are you doing?" she says. "Don't friggin' stop now!"

I smirk against her cheek. "Just tell me what I want to

hear, baby. Your panties were soaked before we ever came in here, weren't they? You loved knowing that you were making me hard in front of everyone, didn't you?"

She digs her nails into my shoulders. "Yes! Now start moving, damn it!"

I chuckle. "Yes, ma'am."

THIRTY-FIVE

DEVYN

I CAN'T BELIEVE THIS is happening right now. We're in a broom closet in a bar! As Riley circles my sensitive bud while simultaneously pumping his fingers, I can't find the will to care anymore. God, I haven't been this excited in ages. Probably since the last time we were together.

There's a small mirror on the opposite wall and I catch site of my reflection. My lips are parted, my breasts rise and fall with each sharp breath, my nipples are tightened into pebbles, and my skin has the telltale flush of arousal.

Riley follows my eyes to the mirror and smiles. "You look like a fucking goddess right now. Do you see how goddamn beautiful you are?" He picks up the pace using a skilled mixture of feather light touches and measured rubs.

"Oh, Rye, I'm so close. Please," I moan.

He adds a second finger and begins to curl them inside of me. "Like this, baby?"

Out of my mind with the desire to come, I lift my hips as

much as possible to match his movements. "YES! Keep doing that!"

The room is quiet except for our heavy breathing and the wet glide of his fingers. Riley thrusts his fingers once more and my orgasm explodes out of me. He continues pumping them in and out while my body clamps down on him. I scream over and over as I come until he slams his hand over my mouth.

"Ssshh," he chuckles. "Someone's going to think I'm murdering you in here."

RILEY

DEVYN SLIDES DOWN MY body after I finished rocking her world with my hand. My eyes never leave hers as I suck her sweet juices off my fingers.

"Mmm, even better than I remember."

She blushes as she sets her clothing back into its rightful position. "I can't believe we just did that! Everybody's going to know what we were up to when we go back out there. Do you think they'd notice if we snuck out the back door?"

I smile. "You want some back door action, huh?"

Her mouth gapes and she smacks my chest. "Oh my God, you're such a pervert!"

I shrug. "I didn't hear you complaining a minute ago."

She smirks. "Uh, no. Definitely not going to complain about that." She looks down to my obvious erection. "You still need to be taken care of. You can't go out there like that."

I step back and adjust myself as she reaches for my belt. "I'll be fine, baby. You can take care of me later. This was all for you."

Her eyes widen. "What? That's not fair."

I grab her hand and open the door. "Trust me; I got plenty of enjoyment out of that. Why don't you head back to the guys? I'm going to wash my hands in the bathroom and I'll be right there."

She blushes even more as she looks down at my hand. "Okay."

When I return to the table, I see Rainey and Devyn at the bar leaning into each other talking. Devyn catches my eye and winks.

Brody gestures towards them. "Now there's some prime spank bank material for you. In my mind, they've already started making out and are tearing each other's shirts off."

I laugh. Okay, admittedly not a bad visual, but there's no way I'm letting this guy masturbate to my girl. "Dude, if you ever mention Devyn's name again while talking about jacking off, I'll kick your ass."

"I second that," Drew growls.

Brody holds his hands up. "Fine, Rainey it is. I have plenty of fantasies in mind for that fine ass woman."

"Yeah, along with every other woman from age eighteen to thirty," I laugh.

"Hey, don't underestimate the power of a hot cougar. I'm definitely not opposed to some Mrs. Robinson action one of these days," Brody says.

I roll my eyes. "I have no doubt, dude."

"Will you Nancys shut the hell up so I can watch the game?" Drew complains.

I tip my beer towards him. "Sounds good to me, man."

THIRTY-SIX

DEVYN

IT'S FRIDAY AND I'M meeting Riley's parents tonight. I'm so nervous despite Rye's repeated assurances that I have no need to be. What will they think of me? Will they be mad at me for keeping Nathan from them all these years? Will they think I'm good enough for their son? And what about Nate? Will he behave? I can't imagine what they'd think if his potty mouth comes out.

As I'm running around my bedroom frantically getting ready, Nathan comes in. He's dressed in a red plaid button up with a pair of little khakis. He looks like a proper young gentleman. Let's hope he acts like one while meeting his grandparents.

"Mom," he extends the word in a whine.

I kneel down and smooth out his hair. "What, baby?"

"My wiener feels funny."

"*What?*" I inspect his pants and they look like they fit fine to me. "What do you mean, buddy?"

He pulls on his pant leg. "My new big boy underpants feel funny."

Ah. Drew insisted on getting him tiny boy boxer shorts. He's been wearing briefs since he was potty trained but Drew insisted that real men wear boxers. I usually defer dude stuff to him so I just went with it.

"Oh, honey, you're just not used to them. Why don't you go take them off and put your other ones on? Hurry up, though, so we're not late."

"All right, Momma."

RILEY

I'M AT THE RESTAURANT with my parents waiting for Devyn and Nathan to arrive. I wanted to pick her up but she insisted on meeting us here so she had a few minutes to freshen up after work before meeting my folks. The poor girl is so nervous. I've assured her that I explained the situation to them and they don't think badly about her *at all*, but she's still uncertain. I know they'll fall in love with her and Nathan instantly. They were so excited when I told them they had a grandchild. I don't think my mom ever thought I'd settle down. As her only child, I was her only hope of having grandbabies to spoil. She would no doubt adore the woman that made that happen.

"What's wrong, honey?" my mom asks.

I check my watch. "They should be here by now."

She chuckles. "Oh, Riley, it's not easy carting around a four-year-old boy. You were a handful at that age. I'm sure the apple doesn't fall too far from the tree. They're only a few minutes late; give them time."

My dad claps me on the back. "Did I ever tell you about

that time you got drunk? You were probably around the same age. Your mother and I were having a get together. You made your rounds and drank a little bit from each beer can that was lying around. We didn't even realize what had happened until you whipped out your itty bitty wee wee and starting peeing on the side of the house, shouting for everyone to look at the pictures you were *drawing*." He laughs. "Ah, those were some good times, huh, Mary?"

I groan. "Christ, Dad. It's a miracle I survived with you two raising me."

My mom rolls her eyes. "Oh, you shush. That was a onetime occurrence. We took great care of you. Boys just have a way of making things interesting. You just wait and see, mister."

I smirk when I think of Nathan and how he definitely keeps things interesting. "For the record, my *wee wee* has grown *quite a bit* since then."

My mom pats me on the cheek. "I'm sure it has, dear. If you take after your father, Devyn is quite the lucky lady."

I cringe. " Mom! Gross! I didn't need to know that!"

She and my dad laugh while I check my watch again. As if I summoned them with my thoughts, Devyn and Nathan walk into the room. My God, she looks amazing. She's wearing a modest black dress but it hugs all of her new curves perfectly. My dick jerks a little when I wonder what she's wearing under the dress. *Calm down, boy.*

I stand up as they approach the table and scoop Nathan into my arms. "Hey, buddy, how are you doing?"

"Daddy, I'm free-balling!"

"Nathan!" Devyn whisper-shouts.

I laugh. "What'd you say, little man?"

"Unca' Drew bought me some big boy underpants but they made my wiener feel funny so Momma said to go put on my regular underpants but I couldn't find 'em so now I'm not wearing *any* underpants! Unca' Drew says that when you run out of underpants on laundry day, you just have to go free-balling!"

My dad coughs to cover his laughter. He stands up and offers his hand to Devyn. "You must be Devyn. It's a pleasure to finally meet you. Riley has told us so much about you. I'm Bill and this beautiful lady is my wife, Mary."

Devyn removes her hand from her face to shake my dad's hand. "I am *so* sorry about that. I'm going to kill my brother."

My mom stands and pulls Devyn into a big bear hug. "Oh, never mind that, honey. You just wait. I have tons of really great stories about Riley for you."

Devyn pulls back and laughs. "I can't wait to hear those."

My parents take their seats. I place Nathan in his chair and pull out Devyn's.

She sits down. "Thank you."

I bend down to kiss her on the cheek. "It's my pleasure. You look incredible."

She shivers. "You're not so bad yourself."

THIRTY-SEVEN

DEVYN

DINNER WAS GREAT. RILEY'S parents are wonderful. I really had nothing to worry about; they were so gracious and lighthearted. I can see why he is the way that he is. Nate fell asleep in the car so Riley carried him upstairs and tucked him into bed before joining me in the living room.

He sits next to me on the couch and kisses my cheek. "You were perfect tonight. My folks loved you."

"I loved them too. I'm so glad they were able to forgive me."

Riley brushes a hair away from my forehead. "There's nothing to forgive, Dev. Stop being so hard on yourself."

I smile. "So...Drew's on shift and won't be home tonight."

He raises an eyebrow. "Oh, yeah?"

I start wringing my hands together. "Yeah. So...I was thinking maybe you'd want to stay the night? I usually don't have sleepovers because I don't want Nate to get the wrong impression. But we're moving in together next week so it's no big deal. Right?

Riley cups my cheek in his hand. "I'd love to stay the night. But you know I don't expect anything to happen, right? I mean, it hasn't been that long since you and Jackson broke up. I don't want you to feel...rushed or anything."

I smile as I pull him off the couch and down the hall into my bedroom. I flip on the lamp and say, "I appreciate your chivalry, Rye. I really do. But the truth is...Jackson and I hadn't been *together* for quite a while before we broke up. And I've been waiting for almost five years to take advantage of you. I'd say it's impossible to rush something that's long over-due. Don't you agree?"

He shuts my bedroom door and turns the lock. "Take advantage of me, huh?"

I laugh. "Oh, yes, absolutely. And I'm going to objectify the hell out of you."

He grabs my face and kisses me hard. When he pulls away he says, "Just remember, turnabout's fair play, Dev."

"I'm counting on it."

Riley and I resume kissing while he walks me backwards towards the bed. He starts untying my wrap dress and suddenly, I feel really self-conscious. My body isn't what it used to be the last time we were together. I try my best to keep in shape but having a child definitely had a permanent effect in some areas. My stomach is flat but not nearly as toned, my hips are wider, and I have a few stretch marks across my lower abdomen and thighs. Why did I turn on the lamp? I wonder if I can figure out a way to shut it off without being too obvious.

RILEY

. . .

I CAN'T BELIVE THIS is finally happening. I'm not going to lie and say I didn't hope tonight would turn out this way, but I certainly didn't *expect* it. My dick does a happy dance in my pants as I unwrap her dress and push it off her shoulders.

I take her in from head to toe. She's wearing a black lace bra with a matching thong. I saw parts of her in the closet the other day but the lighting was so poor I didn't get to truly appreciate it. Her new curves are spilling over the cups of her bra. Hips flare out from a trim waist, giving me a little more to grab onto. She had a fantastic fucking body before, but now...this is fucking perfection. I know I'm biased but I'm sure every hetero guy in the world would agree with me. Right before I kicked their asses for seeing her like this.

She wraps her arms around her waist. "Why are you staring?"

"I didn't think it was possible for you to get more beautiful. It seems I was wrong."

She gasps as I press her into the mattress and begin kissing her neck. "You don't need to sweet talk me, Rye."

I pull back with a frown. "What are you talking about? You asked me a question and I gave you an honest answer—not some cheesy line."

She rolls her eyes. "I'm not stupid, Riley. I know I don't look the same as I did when we were first together. I mean, I try to eat right and exercise regularly but there's only so much that could be done after carrying Nathan."

I sit next to her outstretched body. "Devyn, you're right; you don't look the same. You look *better*. How can you not see that?"

She gasps as I trace my finger along the edge of her bra. "I'm at least fifteen pounds heavier than I used to be."

I squeeze her breast in my hand. "More to love." I slide the lace down and take her nipple into my mouth. I pull back with a pop and say, "What else?"

"Huh?"

I circle her areola with my tongue. "What else do you not like about your body?"

"My stretch marks," she pants. "I hate those."

I run my finger over two tiny silver lines right above her hip. I lower my mouth and kiss them. "These marks are because you carried my son in your body. *Our* son. Nothing could be more beautiful than that."

She tangles her fingers in my hair as I move across her abdomen with my lips. "Oh, Rye."

"Yeah, baby?"

"Your mouth should be illegal."

I smile against her skin. "You think so?"

She nods emphatically. "Uh huh."

I crawl up her body until we're face to face. "Are you sure you're not trying to deflect, Devyn? Because we're not going through with this until you're one hundred percent certain of how sexy you are. How crazed you make me when I look at you. Hell, when I even *think* of you." I suck on the shell of her ear and say, "You are so fucking beautiful. Sexy. Smart. No one has ever turned me on like you do. No one has ever made me feel like you do." I pull back and meet her eyes again. "I love your new curves. I love everything about you. I think I've been *in love* with you since the day we met. You're it for me, Devyn. Do you hear what I'm saying?"

Her eyes get misty. "I do."

I nod once. "Good. Now can we get to the fun part?"

She laughs. "The fun part? What could that possibly entail?"

Her eyes roll back as I brush my knuckles against her core. "I'm not so good with words. I should probably just show you."

She moans. "Mmm, that sounds like a great plan."

Her hands clench the blanket as I lower her panties and

rub my nose against her plump outer lips. She lifts her ass so I can remove her thong. "Mmm," I moan as I inhale her sweet scent. "God, I could eat this pussy all night."

She arches her back as I give her wet slit one long lick. "Riley, please!"

"What do you want, baby?" I pin her hips down into the bed and do it again.

She whimpers. "Please don't tease me, Rye! I've waited too long."

I suck her hard little clit and press it against the roof of my mouth. She screams before she grabs a pillow to muffle her sounds. "You like that?"

"YES!" She squeezes the pillow against her face.

I slide back up her body and remove the pillow. "Are you trying to suffocate yourself?"

She blushes. "We need to be quiet so Nathan can't hear us. I'm finding that awfully hard to do right now."

I dive into her mouth and suck her tongue. Grinding my aching cock against her, I say, "Do you know what else is awfully hard right now?"

She pops the button to my pants. "Lose the pants so we can do something about that." Her nails scrape my ass as she impatiently shoves my slacks and boxers down at the same time.

I climb off the bed to fully remove my clothing. I smirk when I see her watching my every move with her mouth agape. "Like what you see?"

She straightens her spine and moves back against the cushioned headboard. She reaches behind her back and unclasps her bra. She throws it aside and spreads her legs enticingly, putting her pretty pink pussy on full display. Trailing her finger down her soaking wet lips, she says, "I'd rather like what I *feel*. Get over here, Rye."

Fuck. I launch myself onto the bed so fast that I almost overshoot and land my ass on the floor.

Devyn laughs so hard she snorts. "Smooth."

I'm pretty sure I look embarrassed—because I am—but I decide to cover it with redirection. I roughly grab her hips and hook her knees over my shoulders. With zero hesitation, I lick her from end to end, up and down, over and over. I eagerly lap her sweet cream and fuck her with my tongue. She's squirming and moaning and clawing at the bedding. I spread her thighs further and insert two fingers, pumping them in and out. Her juices coat my fingers and leave a wet spot on the bed. I flatten my tongue and trace circles over her clit in time with the pumping of my hand. I look up and almost lose my shit when I see her staring down at me with pure ecstasy in her gaze.

"Oh, Riley! I'm going to come so hard."

"Mmm," I murmur. "Give it to me, baby."

Devyn stiffens suddenly, grabbing my hair and clapping my ears with her thighs. I slow my pace until her limbs relax over my shoulders and kiss a path up her torso until I reach her mouth.

She reaches up and bites my bottom lip. "That was unbelievable."

"You're unbelievable. I feel like the luckiest bastard in the world right now."

She smiles brightly and lifts her hips to meet my erection. "Riley, I need you."

I rub the head of my dick through her lower lips and moan. "Right there with you, baby."

I slip just the tip inside of her and groan. "You feel so good." She arches her back to drive me in further. I slip in easily because she's so fucking wet. Her pussy grips me like an iron fist, holding on tight as I pull out slowly. Fuck, this feels so good. *Too good.* "Shit!" I pull out quickly and sit back on my legs.

Devyn sits up, confusion marring her features. "What's wrong? What just happened?"

I look down at my lap. "No condom. I didn't think to bring any."

She smiles. "It's okay, Riley."

"You have some?" Okay, I definitely don't like the thought of using one of Jackson's leftover rubbers but at the moment, I'll take what I can get.

She shakes her head. "No, I don't. But I have an IUD. My chances of getting pregnant are less than they would be if I were on the pill. And I'm clean. I've only been with one other person besides you and we were safe."

I appreciate the fact that she's not using his name while my dick is wet with her cream. "I'm good too," I say quickly. "There haven't been many since...since you and me. And I've never done this without a condom but I got tested regularly anyway."

She climbs onto my lap and grins. Ever so slowly, she lowers herself onto my cock until I'm balls deep inside of her. "So shut up and enjoy the ride."

My hands grip the mattress behind me for balance. She rides my dick without restraint, swiveling her hips at the tip before slamming back down. "Oh, fuck!"

My self-control completely vanishes as she flexes her internal muscles. I grab her hips and surge upward. Her tits are bouncing in front of my face, tempting me, but I can't stop staring into her eyes as I thrust in and out. I ram into her mercilessly, unable to slow down. My need to mark this woman is blinding. She's taking everything I've got with so much enthusiasm. She's being as quiet as possible but in no way reserved.

I know she's close when she bites her lip and her lids become hooded. "Oh, Rye."

I shift so I'm pressing her back into the mattress and I lift her leg over my shoulder. Fuck, she's so much tighter like this! "Devyn."

Our bodies slap against each other as I drive into her fast and hard. She stiffens beneath me again as her body clenches around my dick. I groan and move faster until I feel my own orgasm building in my lower back. Suddenly, I'm coming with her. *In her.* I glide in and out a few more times until the last pulse of my climax wanes. My arms give out and I fall on top of her. She doesn't seem to notice though.

I pull back and lightly kiss her cheeks, her chin, her nose, and finally her lips. "I love you, Devyn."

She smiles sweetly as a single tear runs down her cheek. "I love you, Riley."

THIRTY-EIGHT

DEVYN

"MMM, GOOD MORNING," I mumble sleepily. I have no clue what time it is but I can see the sun peeking through my bedroom curtains.

Riley presses into me from behind as he continues kissing the back of my neck. "I'm certainly trying to make it one."

I gasp when his fingers roam south and find my sensitive bud. He rubs me with expert precision until I'm a slippery hot mess of pure desire. Just as my body begins to tighten, Riley enters me from behind and we groan in unison. I come apart the second he's inside of me, filling me to the brink. My skin is slicked with sweat as we lazily bump and grind against each other, his lips and hands trailing over me in sweet caresses. I can't help but marvel over how well we fit together. Riley said it once before—that we're so in sync like nothing he's ever known—but this is far more powerful. This is the textbook definition of making love. Riley McIntyre—

the self-proclaimed king of fling—is *making love* to me. I feel it with every fiber of my being.

RILEY

FUCK. THERE IS NO better feeling in this world than when I'm inside this woman. I don't know how I could ever get enough of this. Devyn's pussy wraps around me like the most exquisite vise known to man. My arms are banded around her torso, pulling her back into my chest as I push up into her. I bury my face into the crook of her neck and place my hand over her heart. It's beating rapidly despite our languid pace. I feel like I can't get close enough—if I could shrink myself and crawl inside this woman forever I would. And I mean that in the non-creepiest way possible.

I'm setting the pace, slow and sweet, never wanting this feeling to end. Let's be clear, I'm not normally a slow and sweet kind of guy. I like my sex filthy and sweaty until both partners are gasping for air. Making love is for pussies—literally. But like everything else, sex with Devyn is different. Better. Fucking glorious. I want to bawl like a goddamn baby from the pleasure she makes me feel.

"Oh, Rye," she pants. "Please go faster."

I pull out almost all the way just so I can slide back into her wet heat once again. *Mother fuck.* Devyn reaches behind me and scores her nails into my ass, urging me on. That familiar tingle begins stirring in my balls as she tightens her walls around me.

"Oh God, Dev. Your pussy *is* fucking magical," I say as I pick up the pace. "*Jesus.*"

She laughs and begins moving her hips in time with mine. Our bodies slap together with savage desperation. The only sounds in the room are heavy breathing, the wet glide of our bodies connecting, and a litany of *Oh Gods* pouring from both of our mouths. And a light knocking sound. Where the fuck is that coming from?

Knock. Knock.

As the knocking gets more insistent, I realize exactly where it's coming from. Or *who* it's coming from rather. Fuck. This is not happening. *This is not happening.* I grind into Devyn trying to ignore the little person on the other side of that door. We're both so close. *So fucking close.* Yet so far.

Devyn gasps as my thrusts become more urgent. "C'mon, Riley. He's not going to go away."

"I'm trying," I pant. "Stop talking about the kid. You're making it harder to get there."

She laughs. "This is our life now. You're going to have to get used to it. C'mon already! I'm so close!"

"Will you quit pressuring me?" I gripe. "Geez, I never thought someone would be complaining about my stamina."

"Now's not the time to show off," she pants. "Focus!"

She clenches her internal muscles. "Oh fuck, keep doing that!"

A few more powerful strokes and strategic rubs, and we're both coming together. After several moments, our bodies still.

"MO-OM!!! I'm hungry!" Nathan's knocking has turned into flat out pounding.

Devyn and I laugh as I slide out of her. She climbs out of bed, grabs my discarded shirt from last night and pulls it over her body. "Welcome to parenthood. Where if you're getting any at all, it's usually a race to the finish line."

She waits for me to pull up my pants before opening the door. "Good morning, buddy."

Nate looks into the room with a scowl on his face. "Momma, what took you so long?"

She looks over her shoulder at me. "Sorry, baby; your daddy and I were still sleeping."

"Were you praying in your sleep, Momma?"

Devyn scrunches her face. "What? Why would you say that?"

Nathan shrugs. "Because you kept saying God's name. Christopher says that his mommy and daddy always make funny noises and say God's name a lot when they're sleeping. He said that's because they're praying in their sleep."

"I need to have a talk with this kid's parents," I mutter.

Devyn laughs. "Why don't you go pick out your cereal, honey? I'll be there in just a minute."

"Can I have Unca' Drew's Wucky Charms?"

"Sure," she says. "I won't tell if you won't."

He pumps his fist in the air. "YES! You're the best momma ever!"

I pull her into me as he runs down the hall. "You're incredible."

She leans into me. "You think so?"

I hold her tight and kiss her temple. "I really do."

THIRTY-NINE

DEVYN

MOVING DAY IS FINALLY here. We enlisted everyone's help so the process is much smoother than I would've expected. Nathan keeps running between all three bedrooms while Riley is putting his bed together.

I narrowly miss crashing into my exuberant little boy and lean against the doorframe. "Do you need any help?"

Riley finishes screwing Nate's headboard to the frame and looks up. "No, I'm almost done. I'd love a bottle of water though."

"One water coming right up," I say.

I make my way downstairs and head over to the kitchen. A noise causes me to stop dead in my tracks right before I cross into the room. I listen for a moment and hear muted whispers and a weird smacking sound. I tiptoe around the corner and am frozen by the sight in front of me. Brody has Lorraine pinned against the fridge and she's not protesting in the least. In fact, she happens to be running her fingers over the *crotch* of his jeans.

Brody groans as he presses into her. "Fuck, Rainey. You're killing me."

Lorraine leans into him and kisses him briefly before pulling back. "You know you love it."

He grabs her hips with both hands. "Honey, you know I do. You can touch my dick any time you'd like."

She takes one of his hands and guides it to her breast. "Mmm. I like that idea."

What the heck is happening right now? Oh my God, I can't take this anymore!

I clear my throat. "Hi, guys."

They break apart so fast it'd be comical if I wasn't so freaked out right now.

"Devyn!" Lorraine shouts nervously. "What are you doing here?"

I lean against the island and give them a knowing look. "It's my kitchen. What are *you* doing in here?"

"Uh…" she stammers.

Brody rips open the refrigerator door so hard I'm surprised it doesn't fall off the hinges. "Uh…beer. We came to get beer. Right, Rainey?"

I smirk. "It takes two of you, huh?"

Brody looks between the two of us and apparently decides that flight is the best course of action. "Uh…I gotta go…somewhere other than here."

He quickly shoulders past me and steps out the back door. Lorraine tries to follow but I block her from going anywhere. "Lorraine, what did I just walk in on?"

She blushes. Lorraine *never* blushes. "Depends. How long have you been standing there?"

I cross my arms over my chest. "Long enough."

She rolls her eyes. "It's nothing. We're just having a good time."

"You and *Brody*? How long has this been going on?"

She looks over my shoulder. "I don't know...not long. Please don't say anything, Dev. We don't want to make a big deal out of nothing. We're just scratching an itch. That's all."

I look at her skeptically. "Rainey, that doesn't sound like—"

"Hey, sis, can I fire up the grill now? I'm fucking starving," Drew says.

Rainey takes his interruption as her ticket to end our conversation. She pats him on the back. "Great idea, Drew! I'll help!"

"Sweet!" he says. "You get started on the corn and I'll take care of the ribs."

She busies herself digging through the fridge. "I'm on it."

"Rainey—" I start to say.

She holds her hand up. "Not now, Dev. Drew and I have to feed the natives before they get restless. We'll talk later."

"This conversation isn't over," I warn.

She does an exaggerated eye roll. "Trust me; I know I'm not that lucky."

Lorraine and Drew cook while Brody finishes assembling the patio furniture. I smile when I see Riley and Nathan coming out to join us on the deck.

Nathan holds out a miniature model of a jet. "Mom, look what Daddy gave me! He said I can make planes just like he does when I grow up if I wanna!"

"He doesn't make them," Drew mutters. "He draws pictures of them."

Riley laughs. "Aircraft design is a little more involved than that, dude."

Drew rolls his eyes. "Whatever." He crouches down to Nate's level. "I thought you said you want to be a big strong fireman like your Uncle Drew when you grow up?" He flexes his ridiculously large biceps for emphasis.

Nathan mirrors the move. "I can be a big, strong fireman *and* make planes!"

Riley laughs and ruffles his hair. "You sure can, bud."

Nathan beams. "See Unca' Drew? Daddy says I can!"

Drew stands up and resumes his position at the grill. "Well, if Daddy says it, then it must be true," he says dryly.

I smack Drew's chest. "Behave."

"Yeah, yeah," Drew mutters.

The six of us spend the rest of the evening eating, drinking, and sharing plenty of laughter. I smile to myself as I look around. I'm so lucky to have these people in my life. I couldn't ask for anything more. I keep a close eye on Lorraine and Brody but they're careful not to slip up again. I find myself wondering once again what is going on between those two. Lorraine is certainly open to exploring her sexuality but she doesn't take sex lightly. She says they're just scratching an itch but it's so out of character for her that I have trouble believing that. Why Brody? Why now? She's seen him go through a string of meaningless hookups. Why would she want to get involved with someone like that?

I catch Riley's eye and bite my lip when I realize that he behaved exactly like Brody back in the day. And now look at him. You know that saying that the right person can make anyone change their ways? It took us far too long to figure it out but I've learned that it's certainly true. At least for me and Riley. I don't know what's going on with Rainey and Brody—I just hope that she doesn't get hurt. Things might get a little awkward between me and Riley if I have to remove his best friend's testicles.

Drew sits at the end of my lounger and nods to Riley. "Are you sure about moving in with this schmuck?"

I roll my eyes and laugh. "I'm positive, Drew."

He pouts. "I'm going to miss you guys."

I slide down the chair and pull him into a side hug. "We're going to miss you too. You're always welcome here, you know."

He hugs me tighter. "I'm holding you to that."

RILEY

NATHAN IS ASLEEP AND everyone but Rainey has gone home. I keep fingering the ring box that's been burning a hole in my pocket, thinking about what I want to say to her. I need to make this perfect.

Devyn walks Rainey to the door. "I mean it, Lorraine. We're having a long talk tomorrow."

"Yes, mother," Rainey replies. "Goodnight."

"Night." After locking up, Devyn turns around and surveys the room. "Man, we'll be unpacking these boxes for a while."

I clear my throat nervously. "Uh...yeah. Lots of boxes."

She gives me a strange look. "Are you okay?"

"Come here," I say.

She comes closer and smiles sweetly at me. "What's going on, Rye?"

"I know it might seem fast," I stammer. "But when you think about it, we've known each other for almost ten years. Yeah, we hit some pretty big speed bumps along the way, but we made it through. And now everything's perfect. I have you, and Nathan...this house. We can be a family. There's only one thing that's missing."

She grabs my hand. "Everything *is* perfect. I couldn't possibly ask for anything else."

I shake my head. "See, that's where you're wrong. I can think of one really important thing to ask for."

She crinkles her brows. "What's that?" I drop to my knee

and pull the ring out of my pocket, opening the box. "Oh," she gasps.

I take her hand. "Devyn, I meant it when I said that *you're it for me*. There's never going to be anyone else in this world that means more to me than you do. I've loved you for almost ten years, even though I was too stupid to admit it until recently. But I know, without a doubt, that we were meant to be together. I want to spend the rest of my life with you. I want to teach Nathan how to play football and drive a car. I want to make more babies with you and watch our child growing inside of you. I want to run out at two in the morning to get you pickles and ice cream or whatever other nasty shit pregnant ladies crave. I want to bounce our grand-children on my knee and look over at you when you're old, wrinkly, and gray and still think you're the sexiest woman alive. I want to be there through it all with you. I want to *do* it all for you. For us. There's only one thing I need from you in return."

She wipes a tear away. "What's that?"

I smile. "I need you to say yes. Devyn Summers, will you make me the happiest sonofabitch alive and be my wife?"

She nods. "Yes."

I slide the two carat solitaire on her finger and stand up. "Yes? Really?"

The tears are flowing freely now. "Really, Rye. Now take me to bed so we can practice making those babies."

I grin. "Deal."

Want more of the Dealing with Love crew? Check out Deal Takers, Brody and Rainey's story, and Deal Makers, Drew and Charlotte's story!

ALSO BY LAURA LEE

Dealing With Love Series (Interconnected standalones)

♥Deal Breakers (Devyn & Riley's story)

♥Deal Takers (Rainey & Brody's story)

♥Deal Makers (Charlotte and Drew's story)

Bedding the Billionaire Series (Interconnected standalones)

♥Billionaire Bosshole

♥Billionaire Bossman (Formerly Public Relations)

♥Billionaire Bad Boy (Formerly Sweet Temptations)

Windsor Academy Series (Books 1-3 must be read in order)

♥Wicked Liars

♥Ruthless Kings

♥Fallen Heirs

♥Broken Playboy (Bentley's story-can be read as a standalone)

Standalone Novels

♥Beautifully Broken

♥Happy New You

♥Redemption

Go to: https://www.lauraleebooks.com/subscribe-to-my-newsletter
to sign up for Laura's newsletter and you'll be the first to know
when she has a sale or new release!

ABOUT THE AUTHOR

Laura Lee is the *USA Today* bestselling author of steamy and sometimes ridiculously funny romance. She won her first writing contest at the ripe old age of nine, earning a trip to the state capital to showcase her manuscript. Thankfully for her, those early works will never see the light of day again!

Laura lives in the Pacific Northwest with her wonderful husband, two beautiful children, and three of the most poorly behaved cats in existence. She likes her fruit smoothies filled with rum, her cupboards stocked with Cadbury's chocolate, and her music turned up loud. When she's not chasing the kids around, writing, or watching HGTV, she's reading anything she can get her hands on. She's a sucker for spicy romances, especially those that can make her laugh!

For more information about the author, check out her website at: www.LauraLeeBooks.com

You can also find her "working" on social media quite frequently.

Facebook: @LauraLeeBooks1
Instagram: @LauraLeeBooks
Twitter: @LauraLeeBooks

Verve Romance: @LauraLeeBooks
FB Reader's Group: @Laura Lee's Lounge
TikTok: @AuthorLauraLee

ACKNOWLEDGMENTS

To my husband, Tad: Your unwavering support and encouragement is invaluable. You continue to amaze me every day with all that you do for me and our children. I am truly honored to be your wife. I mean, really, who else would put up with my never-ending sarcasm and eye rolls?

To my children, Kaitlynn and Carter: Thank you for your patience while I lock myself away to write at all hours. You both make me so proud each and every day. Mommy loves you to infinity plus infinity!

To my brother, Mike: Thank you for getting drunk as a toddler and giving me two nephews to use as inspiration for this story.

To Jen (JL) Durfey: Thank you once again for all of your feedback throughout the writing process and your beautiful designs. I really, really, REALLY want to read some more of your stories so get back to writing them, lady!

To Travis Frost: This story wouldn't be nearly as funny without your man-child ways and potty humor. Go shorty, it's your birfday! We gonna party like it's your birfday!

To my beta readers, Jamie Clark-Frost and "Princess" Catania: Thank you once again for allowing me to bounce ideas off of you throughout the writing process. You're two of my favorite ladies alive and I wouldn't trade you for all the books in the world! Anyone who knows me well, knows how powerful that statement is!

To my editor, Erin Potter: Thank you for continuing to put up with my delays, sentence flow issues, and punctuation errors. You're truly a joy to work with and I will happily endorse your services at Shamrock Editing any time!

To all the bloggers and reviewers: Taking time out of your busy lives to share your opinions with others makes it possible for Indie authors like me to do what we love. I can't possibly articulate how valuable you are to me, but please know that I am eternally grateful for everything you do.

Last, but NEVER least, to my readers: If you took the leap with me from paranormal to contemporary romance, thank you for putting your faith in me! I hope you enjoyed this story as much as my previous ones. If you're new here, welcome and thank you for your support! You all made it possible for me to leave a seventeen-year career to pursue writing full time. My life is infinitely better now and I cannot possibly thank you enough for that. I will forever be your fangirl!

Made in the USA
Coppell, TX
02 November 2023

23739595R00154